"What happened to you?"

"While I was in the army overseas, my wife divorced me," Max said. "There was one thing she neglected to tell me." He pulled in a deep breath, held it for a long moment, then released it slowly. "She'd been pregnant with my child."

Rachel's heart twisted like a bundle of barbed wire. "She raised your child without your knowledge?" Who had his child now?

"Not exactly. She put our daughter up for adoption without my knowledge." He backed away, leaning against the counter, his hands gripping its edge.

Suddenly staring into his bleak expression, she knew the answer. Her child. Thirteen years ago. A girl. Could it be? No, that wasn't possible. "Where is she?"

"Here." His gaze clouded as though the sun glittering on the grass had suddenly disappeared.

Her world fell away, the room spinning out of control.

Books by Margaret Daley

Love Inspired

The Power of Love
Family for Keeps
Sadie's Hero
The Courage to Dream
What the Heart Knows
A Family for Tory
*Gold in the Fire
*A Mother for Cindy
*Light in the Storm
The Cinderella Plan
*When Dreams Come True
*Tidings of Joy

**Once Upon a Family
**Heart of the Family
**Family Ever After
A Texas Thanksgiving
**Second Chance Family
**Together for the Holidays
†Love Lessons
†Heart of a Cowboy
†A Daughter for Christmas

*The Ladies of
    Sweetwater Lake
**Fostered by Love
†Helping Hands Homeschooling

Love Inspired Suspense

So Dark the Night
Vanished
Buried Secrets
Don't Look Back
Forsaken Canyon

What Sarah Saw
Poisoned Secrets
Cowboy Protector
††Christmas Bodyguard

††Guardians, Inc.

MARGARET DALEY

feels she has been blessed. She has been married more than thirty years to her husband, Mike, whom she met in college. He is a terrific support and her best friend. They have one son, Shaun. Margaret has been writing for many years and loves to tell a story. When she was a little girl, she would play with her dolls and make up stories about their lives. Now she writes these stories down. She especially enjoys weaving stories about families and how faith in God can sustain a person when things get tough. When she isn't writing, she is fortunate to be a teacher for students with special needs. Margaret has taught for more than twenty years and loves working with her students. She has also been a Special Olympics coach and has participated in many sports with her students.

A Daughter for Christmas
Margaret Daley

Steeple
Hill®

Published by Steeple Hill Books™

STEEPLE HILL BOOKS

Steeple
Hill®

Recycling programs
for this product may
not exist in your area.

ISBN-13: 978-0-373-87631-0

A DAUGHTER FOR CHRISTMAS

Copyright © 2010 by Margaret Daley

www.SteepleHill.com

Printed in U.S.A.

The Lord is good, a stronghold in the day of trouble: and he knoweth them that trust in him.
—*Nahum* 1:7

To Emily Rodmell, my Steeple Hill editor—
thank you for all your hard work.

Chapter One

On his second day in Tallgrass, Oklahoma, Dr. Max Connors opened his front door to discover the one woman he wasn't quite ready to meet. Rachel Howard. Mother of his child.

Although she didn't know that. Yet.

Prim, proper Rachel, with her reddish-brown hair pulled back in a twist, held up a plate full of fudge. "Welcome to the neighborhood."

The smile that graced her full lips transformed her plain features into radiance and needled his conscience. His reason for being in Tallgrass would totally shatter her world.

When he didn't say anything right away, she added in a cultured voice, "I'm part of the welcoming committee for Ranch Acres Estates."

"There's such a thing as a welcoming committee?" In New York City he couldn't have envisioned anything like that. Certainly not in his apartment building where he'd hardly known his neighbors. But then he'd worked long hours at the hospital as an emergency room doctor.

"Yes, especially for the doctor who's going into practice with Dr. Reynolds. I promised Kevin I would give you a proper welcome."

"You know Kevin Reynolds?" He knew she did, that her deceased husband had been Kevin Reynolds's partner, but he couldn't think of anything else to say.

"He's a good friend." She bent a little closer, as though she were imparting a secret. "In case you haven't figured it out, Kevin is very excited you've decided to move to Tallgrass. And wants to make sure you stay around."

A whiff of lavender teased Max's nostrils. "Come in." He quickly stepped back to put some space between them. He hadn't been prepared to meet her in person yet, and her close proximity only reinforced that. "Please excuse the mess." He waved his hand toward the boxes stacked around his living and dining areas. "I've got some of the kitchen put together. Let's go back there."

When Rachel entered the kitchen, she stopped a few feet inside. "You've been here a day, and you've already got this in order. I'm amazed. When I moved into my house, it took me a week to do that."

"I figure if I don't tackle the kitchen this weekend I won't get it done and I love to cook."

"You do? You sound like my granny and my sister, Jordan."

He gestured toward a chair at his round glass table. "You don't like to cook?"

"I do it because I have a family to feed, but I'm not passionate about it like Jordan is." She sank onto the seat and placed her housewarming gift of fudge on the table, her movements precise, graceful.

And for a few seconds they captured his attention. He mentally shook his head and finally asked, "What are you passionate about?" Again, he knew the answer before she said it because he'd made a point to find out as much as he could about the woman raising his daughter.

"Quilting."

"Why?" He took the chair across from her, still needing the distance to keep his perspective. Her photo didn't really do her justice. It'd captured her features but hadn't conveyed the warmth radiating from her, the twinkle in her blue eyes, which reminded him of the color of a lagoon he'd swum in on a rare vacation to Tahiti a couple of years ago between working in the Middle East and New York.

"I love telling a story through a quilt. At church a group of us are working on one that tells the story of Christ. It'll go on the wall in the rec hall, hopefully by Thanksgiving." Her voice conveyed her excitement. About quilting or Jesus? Or both? He knew she was strong in her faith. She attended Tallgrass Community Church, or at least that was what the private detective's report had said.

He forced himself to relax back in his chair, but his gut tightened as though he were preparing for a punch. What was he doing here? Doubts began to assail him about his plan—one that might not have been thought out as well as it should have. What he'd come up with in the safe confines of his apartment in New York City mocked him now. His actions would affect a lot of people. "This fudge looks delicious." He touched the piece closest to him, needing to do something to take his mind off his doubts.

"It's a secret family recipe handed down through the daughters. The first few times I made it I messed it up bad. It was a soft blob of chocolate. It tasted fine, but it didn't set up. Granny had to come to the rescue. A Masterson has to be able to make this fudge, according to her. It's a family tradition. I've been trying to teach my daughter, but she doesn't want to have anything to do with cooking."

Tension whipped down his length. He clamped his jaws together for a few seconds, drew in a deep breath to ease his stiff muscles and said, "How many children do you have?"

"Three. Taylor, my daughter, is thirteen. And I have two boys, twins, who are four."

"That sounds like you've got your hands full."

The gleam in her eyes dimmed. "It isn't easy being a single mom, but I have family here which helps."

"Ah, that would help. Who's giving you problems? The thirteen-year-old or the twins?"

Her chuckles sprinkled the air like powdered sugar. "It's obvious you haven't dealt with a teenager."

He nodded, stamping down his anger simmering beneath the surface. Rachel Howard wasn't at fault, but she could be hurt by his presence in Tallgrass. "Guilty as charged. I haven't had the pleasure other than as a doctor." His deceased ex-wife hadn't given him a chance to find that out. Leaning slightly forward in his chair, he snatched a piece of fudge. "But I have it on good authority they can be a challenge to raise."

"Your source is correct."

"I'll tell my brother he isn't alone in dealing with his teenager."

"Does he live here?"

"No, back in New York—upstate."

"What made you come out here to…" She pressed her hand over her mouth. "I'm sorry. It's none of my business."

"That's okay. I needed a change." Which was true but not the main reason he'd moved to Tallgrass. A prickling of unease in the back of his mind caused him to shift in his chair.

"Well, I know that Kevin is ecstatic no matter what made you decide to take him up on his offer."

Max struggled to keep his expression from showing any hint of his main motive for moving to Tallgrass. To cover the sudden awkward silence, he took a bite of the morsel he held. The chocolate melted in his mouth, offering a burst of sweetness to tempt his palate. "This is delicious. Is there any chance I could get the recipe? I don't normally make desserts, but for this I would make an exception."

Rachel shook her head. "Sorry. My granny would have my head if I passed it on to anyone outside the family." When she smiled, her whole face glowed. "And I'm not brave enough to get on the wrong side of my grandmother."

He laughed. "I've got to meet this woman. Maybe I could persuade her to reveal it."

A serious expression descended but only for a second before the corners of her mouth tilted up again. "This I've got to see. It won't work, but I can't deny you a chance to try."

He finished the rest of the piece of fudge and sucked the last taste off the tip of his finger. "I love a good challenge, and it sounds like your grandmother is one."

"Since you live on the same block and your house is next door to her—beau, as she calls Doug Bateman—you'll probably get your chance."

He couldn't resist picking up another chocolate delight and eating part of it. "This neighborhood is getting more interesting by the minute."

"Tallgrass may be smaller than New York, but we have our own unique characters."

"You'll have to tell me all about my neighbors."

Rachel checked her watch and rose. "I wish I had the time, but I have to pick up my boys from their playtime at the church. But you'll have to come to dinner one evening. I'll have the rest of my family down and introduce you to part of the neighborhood." She started for the foyer, her glance straying to all the boxes stacked along the walls and some even in the middle of the living room. "And it should be soon."

"You don't have to do that." He hadn't gone to a neighbor's house for dinner since he was a child.

She fluttered her hand while saying, "Nonsense," then grasped the handle and opened the door. "That's what neighbors are for. To help out when you need it." Pinning him with an expression that dared him to disagree, she added, "You don't need to spend your time cooking when you have all this to do. How about tomorrow evening? I'll see if Kevin can come, too. We'll consider it your welcome to Tallgrass party."

As she stepped out on to the porch, he clutched the edge of the door. "I can't have you go to all that trouble." *Especially since you don't know why I'm here.*

"You didn't. I volunteered." The blue sparkle in her eyes intensified. "I love giving parties. Just wait until the holidays start next month. I have six weeks of fun."

Was he ready for this? The tapping of his heartbeat increased. "What time tomorrow night?"

"Six." She turned and pointed to the house across the street and down one. "That's where I live."

Yes, I know. "Beautiful place. Your flowers are gorgeous."

"Mums and pansies. I planted them a few weeks ago."

Moving out on to the porch, he surveyed his yard,

the grass almost completely brown now. The few scrubs in front looked pitiful compared to everyone else's on the block. "It's obvious the previous owner wasn't into gardening."

"They weren't, but as long as you don't have junk piled up in the yard and multiple old cars rusting and parked around everywhere, you'll be okay."

"Good. I was getting kind of worried."

"You'll be fine at least until the holiday season. Then it's all-out war to see who has the best decorated lawn."

He dropped his jaw. "Really?" He didn't even put up a Christmas tree. Usually he worked Christmas Eve and Day so others could stay home with their families. He'd wanted a family at one time, but had given up the dream. Now he had a second chance.

She grinned. "No, just kidding." She descended the steps and spun around at the bottom. "Sort of." Then she sauntered down the sidewalk and crossed the street.

He clasped the white railing on his porch and watched her disappear into her house. Nothing had prepared him to meet the woman who'd adopted his child. A child he'd only recently learned about. At first he'd wanted to storm to Tallgrass, demand his daughter back from the family that had her for thirteen years and seek custody of his only child, even if his chances of winning a custody battle weren't good.

Not one word of the detective's report had drawn an accurate picture of Rachel Howard. She was no longer a two-dimensional person on a sheet of paper, but a real-life woman who brought a room to life when she entered. Who exuded graciousness.

All the plans he'd made back in New York City continued to taunt him. He wanted to get to know his daughter, to be a part of her life, but at what cost?

Shoving himself away from the railing, Max swung around and strode into his house. He withdrew his cell from his jeans pocket and punched in his brother's number.

"I'm here." Max's fingers clenched the small plastic phone.

"How's it going? Have you seen her?" Brendan Connors asked, apprehension and a certain edge of excitement in his voice.

"Not Taylor. But I've met Rachel Howard."

"You went over there? I thought you were going to wait and observe them for a while before you made your move. Figure out how best to approach your daughter."

"Rachel came over to welcome me to the neighborhood. Right now I feel like a heel. Do you know what this could do to the woman, to her whole family?"

"Taylor is yours, and she was taken away from you through no fault of yours. You have a right to be her father now that you know about her. The lawyer said you had a case of fraud possibly. It could help you get custody of Taylor."

"The optimal word is *possibly,* and the Howards weren't involved in the fraud. Only my ex-wife. I want to be a part of Taylor's life. I just didn't realize until now how many others will be involved." Max sank on to the couch, weariness enveloping him after a two-day road trip to Tallgrass and what unpacking he'd done so far. He needed some kind of order. He felt as though his life were exploding into hundreds of pieces of shrapnel. In the war, he'd struggled to repair the damage bombs had done to soldiers, sometimes failing. He couldn't fail now.

"Look, if you have to blame anyone for this current

situation, blame your ex-wife. She had your child and gave her up for adoption while you were overseas."

Max could still remember how his wife had told him she didn't want children, especially with him gone all the time. She'd informed him she wasn't ready to be a mother, and maybe he hadn't been because he'd had to work long hours. But that fact hadn't deterred him from wanting a family when he'd married Alicia.

"She divorced you and never told you she was even pregnant, all because she didn't like the fact you had to pay the army back for funding your medical training by working for them. You couldn't help that a good part of that was overseas where she didn't want to go."

Anger infused his brother's voice, reminding Max of his own after he discovered Alicia's deception and betrayal. Brendan had been there to listen. Max would never had known about Taylor if Alicia's younger sister hadn't found the papers about the adoption in Alicia's belongings after she died.

Max hung his head and kneaded the taut cords of his neck. "I can't rush into anything. That much I know. I'll get to know Taylor and the Howard family first."

"That could be dangerous."

"How so?"

"You could begin to care about them and not want to disrupt their lives. Your end goal is trying to get custody of Taylor if at all possible."

He didn't think he had the ability to care deeply for others. It was too painful. He'd lost too many people in his life to risk that again. And yet he wanted to get to know his daughter, be a part of her life. There had been a time in his life when he'd desperately wanted to be a father. He'd given up on that dream—too many tours of duty in hot zones around the world. The things he'd seen had left their mark on his soul.

But Taylor was his daughter—a part of him.

Max straightened, glancing out the window at Rachel's house. "I'll come up with something." His hand ached from holding the cell so tightly. "I need to go. I wanted to let you know I arrived."

"Keep me posted."

"Will do."

Max clicked off his cell and stuffed it back in his pocket. After scrubbing his hands down his face, he massaged his fingertips into his temple. Tomorrow night he would meet his daughter for the first time. A tight band about his chest threatened to squeeze the breath from him. He forced oxygen-rich air into his lungs. The realization that months of searching and planning had finally come to an end unnerved him more than patching up a soldier under enemy fire.

Pausing in the doorway of the den later that day, Rachel watched her two sons playing with their Legos. After several years of trying to have a child, she and Lawrence had ended up adopting Taylor. When their daughter was five, they started talking about adopting another child. They both wanted more children. They had begun the adoption process again when she'd become pregnant with twins.

Sam was her creative child, diving right in and coming up with things as he went, while Will had to figure out everything before he started. They approached life from opposite ends, and yet they were so close. Their father's unexpected death two and a half years ago hadn't affected them. They had been too young to realize what had really happened to their dad.

Not like Taylor. She'd been Daddy's little girl and had dreamed of becoming a doctor just like her father. Now all she wanted to do was rebel against any authority, especially her mother and the school. It had gotten so bad that Rachel had told her sister she was going to look into homeschooling and she had. It might be just what Taylor needed to do better in her academics. Certainly, the status quo wasn't working.

The chimes of the doorbell echoed through the house. Rachel swung around and made her way to the foyer. It must be Dr. Nancy Baker. The Tallgrass Community College education professor was stopping by on her way home to give her some information on how to start homeschooling.

Rachel opened the front door. The sight of a police officer who attended her church standing there with her daughter next to him stole her breath and greeting.

"I found Taylor in the alley behind the arcade downtown, Rachel. It looks like she skipped school again."

"The school hasn't called me yet."

"I don't think she was at the arcade long."

Rachel peered at Taylor, her head down, her arms and legs crossed, her mouth set in her usual frown. Her soft, short blond hair was now full of gel and sticking up all over. Heavy makeup, especially around her dark green eyes, covered up her olive complexion and made her face look pasty. This was not the way she'd looked when she'd left that morning.

"Thank you, Dan. I'll call the school and let them know Taylor's here."

Taylor pushed through the entrance and stomped toward the stairs. "I'm going to my room."

The sound of her pounding footsteps bombarded

Rachel with her child's anger, always ready to erupt at a second's notice. She sighed.

"I'm sorry about this, Rachel. I know you're worried."

"Was she with anyone else?"

"No, but I think she was getting ready to sneak into the arcade from the back door. I'm going back to check it out, make sure no other kids are there skipping school." Dan tipped his hat and left.

As the police officer descended the porch stairs, her new neighbor from across the street came up the sidewalk. Worry knitted his forehead, his mouth pressed into a firm line.

"Is everything all right? I noticed the patrol car out front and was concerned something was wrong." Max's husky bass voice shivered down her spine. There was something about its sound that commanded a person's attention.

The appeal in his green-colored eyes touched her. For over two years since her husband's death, the situation with her daughter had worsened until she didn't know what to do anymore. "Taylor skipped school—again."

"Again?" He planted himself in the doorway, his large presence filling the entrance as though he could really help her with Taylor.

"Yeah. Third time since the beginning of school. Dan brought her home twice. Once I had to go out and find her."

"What does she say?"

"Not much and that's what's so frustrating." Rachel moved to the side. "Come in. No use for you to stand on the porch. Do you want some coffee? I keep a pot on all day. I know I drink too much caffeine." As she led him back toward the kitchen, she heard herself chattering a nervous prattle. What a first impression she and her family had made on the new neighbor.

"I drink too much coffee, too."

She poured two mugs and sat across from him at the oak table, sliding his toward him. "I think I know what's going on, but so far I haven't been able to reach her."

"What?"

His calm facade wrapped about her, soothing her tattered nerves. "She's never accepted her father's death. After his passing, she started changing. She used to be so open. Now she keeps things inside. I realize as a teenager that can be typical, but in Taylor's case I don't think so. Then on top of that she's having a lot of problems in school. Her teachers complain she can't sit still. She's always talking when she shouldn't. This year has been especially bad. Her last antic was starting a food fight in the cafeteria."

"How are her grades?"

"As you'd expect, not good. She's passing two classes by the skin of her teeth. I tried a tutor, and she wouldn't cooperate with the woman. She's smart. In elementary school she had pretty good grades. She rarely got in trouble. I've been thinking of trying homeschooling with her."

"Homeschooling? Kevin said something about a science class he teaches at the office twice a week for some students from Helping Hands Homeschooling Group."

"Yeah. I'm hoping to hook Taylor up with him. He's been our family doctor for years."

"Have you talked with him about checking to see if Taylor has something like Attention Deficit Disorder with Hyperactivity?"

"ADHD?" Rachel cupped the mug between her hands,

needing its warmth to melt her chill. "No, I haven't. Why do you think she might have that?"

"Impulsive, can't sit still, trouble in school. It's a possibility."

"Why haven't any of her teachers said anything?"

"That I can't answer. She's in middle school now and probably has six or seven different teachers so it's harder to notice. A doctor has to diagnose it. If it's not that, Kevin should still check her out to make sure there isn't an underlying health reason for the behavior change."

"Hyperactive?" Rachel rubbed her chin. "I know she's always moving, but she can sit still when she wants. She'll watch her favorite TV show and not move an inch. Or she'll play a game on the computer and be engrossed to the point she doesn't even hear me come into the room."

"ADHD kids can be super-focused on something they're really interested in. If they aren't interested, it's very hard to keep their attention." Max took a sip of his coffee.

"How come you know so much about it?"

"My brother has it and his son does, too. Once a parent understands what's wrong, it helps in working with the child. There are certain things that can be done."

The fingers about her mug were still cold as though it had seeped deep into her bones. "If I decide to home-school her, is it something I can do?"

"Sure. I have a book about ADHD. I'll dig it out and give it to you to read."

Lifting her drink, she locked gazes with him. "I've got some thinking and praying to do. I appreciate your input. I'm at my wit's end. I don't know what to do anymore."

He smiled, the crinkles at the sides of his dark green eyes deepening. "I hope it helps you."

"So do I." Rachel sipped her coffee, a visual link between them.

"Who are you?" Taylor asked from the doorway into the kitchen, her attention riveted on Max.

Chapter Two

At the sight of his daughter, Max tensed. His heartbeat thundered in his ears, drowning out what Rachel said to Taylor. All he could see was that the young girl looked just like his ex-wife, except the child had his green eyes. The same shape, long lashes. Until now he'd only seen a picture of Taylor, but it had been grainy, from a distance. The fact that Taylor was a mixture of him and Alicia further disconcerted him.

Rachel fixed her gaze on Max. "This is our new neighbor. He'll be working with Dr. Reynolds."

"Taking Dad's place?" Taylor folded her arms over her chest.

Her words cut through the haze about his thoughts. Pierced his heart. "It's nice to meet you." This was his daughter. One denied him for years. He willed a smile to his face, but his lips quivered from the strain of trying to maintain a nonchalant front. Nothing felt blasé from the lump in his throat to the knot in his gut.

"Are you gonna be in Dad's office?"

Although the question was directed at him, Rachel hurriedly said, "Hon, Dr. Reynolds needs help. The practice is too much for one man."

"But—but…" Taylor snapped her mouth closed and stabbed her mother with a fierce expression. Tears filled her eyes.

Max started to rise, the urge to comfort stronger than his common sense.

Rachel beat him to his feet. "Honey, no one can take your father's place."

But I'm your dad. The words lodged themselves in his throat, choking off his breath. With his teeth gritted, he remained seated and forced air into his lungs while Rachel made her way toward Taylor.

The teenager backed away and spun around. Her footsteps quickly receded.

Rachel pivoted. "I'm sorry. I need to talk with her."

"Go. I understand."

When Rachel disappeared, Max sank back in the chair. His hand shook as he lifted the mug to his lips. For a few seconds, he'd wanted to shout the truth at Taylor and Rachel. But immediately as the urge inundated him, he knew that would be the worst thing to do. Taylor was fragile emotionally and the news could do so much damage. As much as he wanted to be a father, he would not do it at the cost of his daughter's emotional well-being. He had to think about when and how—nothing rash.

Rachel pushed open the door. An empty bedroom greeted her. Where was Taylor? She'd heard her stomping upstairs.

Then a noise drifted to her. Rachel stepped farther inside and tilted her head, listening. The sobs came from the closet. Taylor hadn't hidden in there for over two years. The last time was when she'd first heard the news that her father had died. Rachel moved toward the door that stood ajar a few inches and pulled it toward her.

In the darkness Taylor huddled in her comforter wrapped around her. She clasped it and her legs to her body. When the light from the bedroom invaded the closet, Taylor lifted her head for a few seconds, then curled farther in on herself and continued to cry.

The sound ripped through Rachel, leaving her defenseless in the wake of her child's sorrow. She knelt next to Taylor and laid her hand on her daughter's arm. "Taylor, no one is trying to erase your father's memory. No one can take away the fact he was your dad and a special man. Dr. Reynolds needed help, and Dr. Connors has decided to join him. When your father died, it left a hole in the medical community in Tallgrass that needed to be filled."

Tear-glistening eyes trapped Rachel. "You've forgotten him. You don't talk about him anymore."

Rachel touched her wedding ring. "I haven't taken this off since the day he put it on my finger."

Taylor blinked and swiped her hand across her cheek. Her daughter stared at the diamond pear-shaped solitaire welded to Rachel's platinum band, confusion in Taylor's gaze for a few seconds. "I miss him, Mom. I used to go to his office with him every Saturday. Why did God take him away? I still…" Her words evaporated, leaving only silence.

"Oh, honey." Rachel sat close to her daughter and wound her arms around her. "I've asked myself that very question, but for His own reasons the Lord took your dad home to live with Him. I don't always understand His plans, but He knows best. I used to fight the Lord on His plans for me, but I've learned it's wasted energy." She raised Taylor's chin so her daughter looked directly into her eyes. "That doesn't mean I don't miss your father. I do. I'll always love him."

Taylor went into Rachel's embrace and nuzzled her cheek against Rachel's shoulder. "I'm sorry about today. I just couldn't stay in class another minute."

"Why? What's going on?" Brushing her child's hair behind her ear, Rachel cherished the moment Taylor was in her arms. It had been so rare of late.

"It was science. I hate science. I…" She ducked her head down.

"What if I tell you I'm thinking of homeschooling you? How would you feel about that?"

"Like Nicholas? But he's so smart. I'm not."

Rachel's nephew was a genius, but she had to make her daughter see she was smart, too. "Homeschooling can be for any kid who'll benefit from it. The beauty of it is that we'll go at your pace. If there's something you aren't getting, then we'd spend more time on it." She cupped Taylor's face. "But most important, you are not dumb."

Taylor bent back and stared at Rachel. "Do we have to do science?"

She suppressed a grin. "We have to cover the same subjects as all the kids your age, but the curriculum would be tailored to you and even to your interests. I've been talking with your aunt and Dr. Baker. I think it's something we should try unless you're dead set against it." She'd realized almost from the beginning if Taylor didn't want to do it, homeschooling would never be a success. She had to get her daughter to buy into it.

"No more getting up at six-thirty?"

"We'll have a schedule but not as strict as a school's. If you do better in the late morning, then we'll start later."

"I like singing. I'd miss chorus and drama class."

"Have you thought about joining the choir at church?"

"I'm only thirteen."

"So. There isn't an age restriction. And there's a community playhouse we could look into."

"You've given this a lot of thought."

Rachel nodded. "You mean everything to me."

Tears returned to glimmer in Taylor's eyes. "Can I think about it? I don't want to lose my friends."

"We can make sure you stay in touch with them. Talk with Ashley, Nicholas's cousin. She's close to your age and being homeschooled."

Her daughter sucked in a ragged breath. "I'll think about it."

"Good. I'll let the school know where you are." Rachel rose and backed out of the closet.

Taylor remained, the comforter cuddling her in its soft confines.

This was one of those times it was best to leave her daughter alone for a while. Hopefully, she would think about homeschooling and decide to try it.

Downstairs in the hallway, Rachel picked up the phone on the table and called the school. After reporting that Taylor was at home, Rachel headed to the den and checked on her twins then made her way to the kitchen to decide what to fix for dinner. She came to a stop a few feet into the room.

Max still sat where she'd left him, sipping his coffee. His gaze transfixed hers. "I didn't want to leave until I knew everything was all right. Your daughter seemed pretty upset when she took off out of here."

The intensity in his eyes—as if no one else mattered—hastened her pulse to a faster pace. "I think she's okay.

She responded better than I thought she would when I first went into her room."

"I know we haven't known each other long, but I'm a good listener if you need someone to talk to."

Rachel glanced at the clock on the wall. "We've known each other less than three hours."

"I hate seeing someone hurting."

"That must be why you became a doctor."

"Yeah," he murmured, drank the last swig in his mug and stood. "Thanks. You might not like to cook, but you sure make a great cup of coffee."

"My sister's influence. When she came back to Tallgrass a few months ago, that was the first thing she taught me. She declared mine could grow hair in places a woman wouldn't want."

He chuckled. "That sounds like someone serious about her coffee."

"Among other things." He came abreast of her and suddenly the large kitchen seemed to shrink. "Thanks for your advice concerning Taylor. I'll talk with Kevin. I need answers if there are any."

"If I can help, let me know." He smiled, a sparkle in his green eyes. "After all, we're neighbors now, and I've got it on good authority neighbors help each other—at least in Tallgrass."

"You're a quick learner."

He strode into the entry hall and turned before leaving. "See you tomorrow evening." His gaze fastened on to something behind Rachel.

"Yes, six." She glanced over her shoulder to find Taylor standing at the top of the stairs, a frown slashing her brows downward. When Rachel returned her attention to Max, a shadow clouded his gaze until he realized she was looking at him.

He focused on her, a twinkle dancing in his eyes. "I'm looking forward to meeting the rest of your family, especially your grandmother." Swinging around, he left.

Aware her daughter was coming down the steps, Rachel observed Max for a few extra seconds—taking in his long strides, his jeans that fit snugly over slender hips, the dark brown, almost black, hair that teased his nape with curls—before shutting the door.

"What's happening tomorrow at six?"

Rachel faced Taylor. "A little dinner party."

"With the family?"

"Yes, as well as Mr. Bateman and Dr. Reynolds."

Her daughter nodded toward the street. "Why is he coming?"

"He's the guest of honor."

"Why?"

"I guess because he's new in town. Just trying to help a neighbor."

Taylor's eyes narrowed, her mouth pinched. With a snort, she spun on her heel and headed toward the den. When her daughter disappeared from view, Rachel hurried into the kitchen to call Kevin and set up an appointment for Taylor as well as ask him to dinner. She needed answers. She needed help with Taylor.

"So, tell me about your new neighbor." Jordan put the salad into the refrigerator on Saturday evening right before six. "There have been new ones to the street before, and I don't remember you having a party for them."

Rachel fisted her hand on her waist. "What are you implying?"

"Since he's coming by himself, I figure he isn't married. Is he?"

"No mention of a wife. No wedding ring." No indication he had one when she talked with Kevin about him yesterday.

"That doesn't mean anything. Look at you. You're still wearing yours." Her younger sister gestured toward her left hand.

Rachel peered down at her platinum band. "I don't have a good reason to take it off."

"You wear it to keep men at a distance."

"Just because you're newly married doesn't mean everyone wants to be."

"Is he cute? Nice?"

"I guess he's good-looking."

"Guess! What does that mean? He is or he isn't."

"Okay, he's handsome, rugged like Zachary. By the way, your husband doesn't mind grilling the steaks, does he?"

"He's already with Doug and Kevin bonding over the grill, and they don't even have the steaks yet." Jordan walked to the bay window that overlooked the deck. "Do you think Granny and Doug will get married?"

"I sure hope so, or our mother is going to have a heart attack." Rachel lifted her glass of iced tea and took a sip.

"Maybe we should try fixing Mom up with a man, then she wouldn't be so concerned about what Granny is doing."

Rachel nearly choked on the drink. Coughing, she managed to set the tumbler on the counter before she dropped it. "What is this? You had a fit when Granny and your son were matchmaking with you and Zachary."

"But it worked. We're married. Two weeks by the way."

"So you want to marry Granny, Mom and me off because you are?"

Jordan blushed a deep red. "Being married has some nice benefits."

"I know. I was happily married once." She missed Lawrence and didn't think there was a man who could replace him in her heart.

"So tell me about Dr. Max Connors."

The doorbell rang. "Why don't you go let him in?"

"Sorry. Can't. I'm gonna check up on my husband. We wouldn't want him getting the grill too hot for the steaks. I don't care for meat charred on the outside and red on the inside."

Her sister fled the kitchen so fast Rachel's head spun. She rushed toward the foyer and came to a stop when she spied Taylor letting Max into the house, a bouquet of flowers in his hand. She hung back to see what her daughter would say.

Max smiled at Taylor. "Hi. It's nice to see you again."

Her daughter huffed. "Yeah, well, Mom's in the kitchen. I think you know the way." She turned, caught sight of Rachel and frowned. For half a minute she remained still, then shook her head and hurried up the stairs two at a time.

"Taylor!" Rachel stepped into the foyer. When her daughter halted at the top and peered over her shoulder, Rachel added, "That's no way to greet a guest."

"He's your guest."

Rachel's mouth fell open at the rude behavior of her daughter. What was going on? She started to say something to Taylor, but she vanished down the hall before the words could form in her mind. "I'm sorry. I'll talk to her later."

"Don't worry about it." He presented the bouquet to her. "These are for you."

She took a deep breath of the sweet fragrance from the day lilies, daisies and tiny purple blooms. "Thanks, I love flowers."

"I got that impression from the ones you have in your yard."

"Yeah. The lack of flowers in the winter is one of the reasons I don't like cold weather. But it sure makes me appreciate spring. Come into the kitchen and I'll get a vase for them, then we can make the rounds and I'll introduce you to everyone."

In the room she withdrew a crystal vase from the cabinet and arranged the flowers in it, then put them on the kitchen table. She glanced out the bay window and saw Kevin, Zachary and Doug standing near the grill talking. Jordan was nowhere to be seen.

"Can I help you with anything?"

Rachel paused in pulling the platter of steaks out of the refrigerator. She wasn't used to hearing that. When Lawrence had been alive, she had done everything for the family. And she still did now. "No, I've got things under control. My brother-in-law will grill these." She held up the plate and shut the fridge's door with her hip. "The men immediately escaped outside on the deck. Granny, Mom and Jordan are in the den with the twins and Nicholas, my nephew. I thought you might like to join the men."

"Are you trying to keep me away from Granny?" he asked, his mouth lifting in a lopsided grin.

"I'm trying to spare you the disappointment."

Out on the deck Rachel handed Zachary the meat. "This is Max Connors. My brother-in-law, Zachary, and my grandmother's—friend. Doug Bateman is the one I told you lived next door to you."

Max shook hands with first Zachary then Doug and

finally Kevin. "It's good to meet you two and to see you again, Kevin."

After putting the steaks on the grill, Zachary set the plate down on the wooden table. "Kevin was telling us you're going into practice with him, that you'll start on Monday. What made you decide on Tallgrass? Coming from New York City, I would imagine you're going through a culture shock."

"I haven't had time to. Still trying to get my house in order before I start work."

Kevin slapped Max on the back. "I've warned him he'll be busy from the get-go."

"I know what it means to move. I had to move Jordan's stuff to my home a couple of weeks ago. She hadn't even bothered to unpack all her boxes from when she came to Tallgrass in August. We're still trying to find places for her things. I'm thinking of building on to my house." Zachary picked up the large fork to check the meat.

"How long until the steaks will be done?" Rachel asked, glad to see Max relaxing with the men.

"Ten minutes. If you need more time, I can give you an extra five."

"No, that should be enough." Rachel started to go back into the house.

"I can help."

She stopped at the door and glanced at Max, who suddenly appeared right behind her. "You don't have to. You're the guest of honor."

His gaze snagged hers. "I want to."

His intent look snatched her breath. "Fine. I can always use an extra pair of hands."

In the kitchen she took the plates and glasses down from the cabinet. "I've got everything done but setting the tables."

"Tables?"

"I have my large one which sits eight and then a card table for the four kids."

He carried the dishes toward the dining room and set the plates on each maroon place mat while Rachel came behind him and put the tumblers down. Working side by side, Rachel fell into a rhythm with Max and in ten minutes everything was laid out for dinner.

She moved away. "Thanks. I had more to do than I thought." Angling toward him, she nearly brushed up against him. With a quick step back, she said, "If you need help unpacking tomorrow afternoon, I'm available after church." The words tumbled from her mouth without her really considering them. But the offer felt right.

"You don't have to do that."

"No, just like you didn't have to help me set the table. I want to. Two people are better than one. I can take items out of the box and you can put them away. It'll go twice as fast."

An unreadable expression flashed across his face.

"I wouldn't have offered if I didn't want to help."

A slow smile transformed his neutral features. "Then I accept."

"Good. Now I need to go get Taylor for dinner."

"I can let the others know."

"That would be great."

Rachel strode to the staircase and mounted the steps. The feel of his gaze on her burned a path down her length. She chanced a peek at him when she reached the top. Their gazes connected for a brief moment before her grandmother's voice penetrated the silence. Rachel hurried down the hallway toward her daughter's room.

She eased the door open and found Taylor stretched out on her bed with her back to her. "Dinner is ready."

"I'm not hungry."

Rachel covered the distance to Taylor and sat beside her, laying her hand on her shoulder. "You're going to come down to dinner, and you're going to apologize to Dr. Connors. You're behavior was rude and unacceptable."

Her daughter curled her legs up and clasped them. "I know. I was mad at Cindy."

"Why?"

"I wanted her notes for the science test. She thinks I'm dumb. I'm not." Taylor's voice caught on a sob. "I just have trouble sometimes. The teachers move too fast for me when they're explaining."

"Honey, remember what we talked about yesterday. It's your call if you want to try homeschooling because if we do it I want it to be a partnership between you and me."

Taylor twisted toward her. "I know. Let me see how school goes this week. I'm gonna try real hard to pay attention and listen."

"Fine. Ready to come downstairs?"

"I'll be there in a sec."

Rachel headed back to the dining room as everyone came to the table. Granny sat at the end with Doug next to her. Her mother took the chair beside her grandmother. Kevin held it out for Mom and scooted it in for her. A faint hint of color blushed her mother's cheeks, and she looked away from their family doctor. Interesting. Kevin and her mother were only a few years apart. Rachel hadn't seen her mom reacting like that since her husband left her to raise two children on her own.

Zachary and Jordan seated themselves beside each other while Max helped Rachel into the chair at the head of the table. As he pulled out his seat, Taylor came down the stairs. Her daughter walked over to him, avoiding eye contact until he sat and peered up at her.

Taylor looked directly into his gaze and murmured, "I'm sorry about earlier," then whirled around and quickly took her place at the card table.

Max leaned toward Rachel, his lime-scented after-shave lotion vying with the aromas of the steaks. "What did you say to her?"

"We talked about how she should behave. For the time being, she was willing to listen. Tomorrow may be a totally different day. The hard part of all this is I can remember what it was like to be thirteen." That was the year her father walked out on the family and had left her devastated. She'd been furious at her own mother, but now she understood what it was like to raise children by herself, to make all the decisions and not know if they were correct or not.

"Understanding is the beginning of a solution."

"I hope so because I sometimes feel I'm out of my element."

Chapter Three

Rachel feels out of her element? Max shifted away from her at the dining-room table. That was exactly how he felt. He wasn't equipped to be both a mother and father to his daughter. The more he was around Rachel and Taylor, the more he realized he had to weigh his options carefully concerning what he planned to do in the long run. He wanted what was best for Taylor above all else. Right now he knew he couldn't tell anyone who he was—not while his daughter was too emotionally fragile. Did that mean he had to wait until she grew up? Did the child even know she was adopted?

The thought jolted him with the delicate balance he would have to live with in the coming days. When he had discovered he had a child, he'd wanted to shout it from the rooftops. Keeping quiet would be one of the hardest things he ever had to do. And he would for the immediate future.

After Rachel said a prayer over the meal, she began passing the food around the table. While he took a scoop full of the broccoli-cheese casserole, he peered at Taylor seated with her brothers and cousin. She cut up the pieces of meat for both Sam and Will, laughing at a silly joke Nicholas told them. His daughter ruffled one of the twins' hair, then poured a glass full of milk for the other. Seeing her with her younger brothers nailed home how complicated the situation was, and yet he couldn't squash the yearning to be a father to her.

"Max, what do you think of Tallgrass so far?" Rachel's grandmother handed the bowl with scalloped potatoes to Doug.

"I grew up in a small town in upstate New York. Being here has brought back fond memories of those times." Times he'd forgotten.

"So you really aren't a big-city guy?"

Rachel's voice with a lilting edge to it drew him around to look at her. "I lived in New York City for two years, but before that I was a doctor in the army. I was stationed in various places around the world, sometimes working out of a tent in a makeshift hospital in the middle of nowhere."

"What did you do at the hospital in New York?" Rachel's mother, Eileen Masterson, asked as she cut into her steak.

"Emergency medicine."

"Then Tallgrass will be dull compared to what you're used to." Zachary exchanged a glance with his wife.

But little did they know that was one of the reasons he'd decided to take Kevin up on his offer. He wanted normal after having years of anything but normal. He needed some kind of purpose rather than just going to work and coming home to fall asleep exhausted. "I wouldn't say the word *dull*."

Jordan playfully punched her husband in the arm. "Look who's talking about dull. Your life has been anything but dull. Trying to ride a bucking bull for eight seconds isn't a stroll in the park."

"I've given up my dangerous ways." Zachary winked at Jordan.

She turned to Max. "Don't believe a word he says. I found him the other day riding a horse that wasn't thrilled about having a rider on his back."

Max looked at Jordan. "I can't imagine being on the back of a bucking bull or horse."

"Neither can I. That's what I keep telling my husband."

"I think it would be fun." Taylor speared a piece of meat and added, "Nicholas and I have talked about helping you break the horses." Then she popped the steak into her mouth.

"No," Rachel and Jordan said at the same time.

Max swiveled his attention from Jordan to Rachel. Her eyes huge, she went pale.

"You two don't need to worry. I won't let them. Besides, usually when you 'break a horse,' it doesn't involve any bucking." Zachary brought his fork to his mouth.

"I'm gathering from this conversation you live on a ranch." Max directed the question toward Zachary, realizing there was so much he still needed to discover about his daughter's extended family. The private detective's report only covered so much.

"Yep, I raise horses, train certain ones for the rodeo circuit."

Doug clanged his spoon against his glass. "I've got an announcement. I can't keep quiet another second."

Max, along with everyone in the room, peered at the older man, who pushed himself to his feet and looked at Rachel's grandmother.

His next-door neighbor took Helen's hand. "We're

getting married in two weeks. I wanted to do it next week, but she wanted some time to plan her wedding."

For a moment, silence dominated the room.

Then Taylor hopped up from her chair, came to her great-grandmother and threw her arms around her. "Granny, can I be your maid of honor?"

All at once everyone erupted into congratulations except for Rachel's mother.

She gripped the edge of the table. "But you need someone to take care of you."

Helen stabbed a sharp look at her daughter. "I'm capable of taking care of myself. Remember I'm your mother, not your child. And yes, Taylor, you can be my maid of honor."

"Can I be the best man?" Nicholas asked.

Doug laughed. "Why not."

Rachel stood and raised her glass. "May you two be as happy as Lawrence and I were for many years to come."

The wistful tone of Rachel's voice stirred a longing in Max. He quickly tamped down any emotions because he'd only come to Tallgrass to get to know his daughter. Nothing else could interfere. Especially Rachel.

"Here. Here." Jordan clinked her tumbler against Helen's.

Making himself relax back against his chair, Max studied the excited faces of the people around him. Family. He'd forgotten what it meant to be part of one. He'd been on his own for so long and only in the past few years had joined his brother's family occasionally during a holiday. And then as now, he felt like an observer, watching but never really participating although Brendan was his sibling.

For that matter, what was it like to have a happy

marriage? His to Alicia certainly hadn't been for long. She'd made it clear she wanted something he couldn't give her.

"I knew Doug and Granny would get married. This is great." Jordan took the plate from Rachel and put it in the dishwasher later that evening.

"Did you hear Mom?" Rachel grabbed a pan and rinsed it off before passing it to her sister.

"Kinda hard not to. What's she worried about, really?"

"I think being alone. When Granny moves out, she'll be by herself again."

"Then we need to do something about it."

Rachel stared at Jordan. "And just what do you suggest?"

"Fix her up with Kevin. Did you see how she kept looking at him and blushing?"

"No." She'd been too busy watching Max. He'd fit right in with the family, even to the point of teasing Granny about her top-secret fudge recipe. "I don't know if that's such a good idea. Mom hasn't been interested in dating for quite a while. Just because you're deliriously happy with a man doesn't mean that'll work for someone else."

"Who are we talking about, Mom or you?"

Heat scored Rachel's cheeks. "Mom, of course. I'm not lonely. I have three kids. I had a good marriage and can't see anyone replacing Lawrence."

"You're young. Thirty-six. You've got a lot of years ahead of you. Years when your children will be gone."

"Nothing's worse than a recently married woman wanting everyone around her to be the same."

Jordan shut the dishwasher and turned it on. "What's wrong with being happy?"

"Nothing. I am."

Her sister clasped her arms, forcing her to face Jordan. "Are you? There used to be a sparkle in your eyes. It's gone."

Rachel wrenched free. "That's because my husband died two and a half years ago. My only goal now is to raise my children the best I can."

"You know you can talk to me about Taylor."

"I know. I told her about homeschooling yesterday. She's considering it."

"It's been great for Nicholas. Becca and I coteach sometimes since we live so close now."

"I'm glad you have Zachary's sister nearby." Even to her own ears loneliness laced each word.

"Remember I'm not too far away. Twenty minutes."

Twenty minutes could be a long distance when she was hurting, but Rachel kept that to herself. She had her mother and grandmother living on the same street.

And Max. That thought crept into her mind and wouldn't leave. Was it because he was a doctor like Lawrence? Taking her deceased husband's place at Tallgrass Medical Complex? No, there was something she'd glimpsed yesterday—a hint of vulnerability in his green eyes. It had been reinforced today at dinner.

She shook her head, not sure where that had come from. She'd always been good at reading people, and he gave off vibes—as if he'd been hurt in the past and the wound hadn't healed. She'd been hurt, too. Not by Lawrence but her father. She didn't even know where he was.

Rachel washed down the sink. When she turned from it, she spied Max in the doorway, studying her. That flash of vulnerability flared for a second in his expression and vanished.

He smiled. "I thought I'd better be heading home. I've got a lot of work to do tomorrow if I'm going to start on Monday with Kevin."

"Yeah, I'd better go round up my crew and leave, too. See you at church, Rachel." Jordan strolled from the kitchen, glancing back over her shoulder with a small grin playing at the corners of her mouth.

Leaving her alone with Max. Rachel draped the washcloth over the sink, then closed the space between them. "Don't forget I'll be over to help you tomorrow afternoon."

"I appreciate it."

For half a minute, silence reigned between them. Rachel couldn't pull her gaze from his. Heat returned to flush her cheeks. She swallowed several times, trying to come up with something to say. Finally she blurted out, "Did you get the recipe from Granny yet?"

He chuckled. "Nope, but not from lack of trying. She's a tough cookie."

"That she is. You won't be able to crack her."

"I have the time. I could wear her down."

"I want to be there the day she gives it to you."

"You can have a front-row seat."

"You seem awfully sure of yourself."

A frown furrowed his forehead. "I was taught to make decisions and be sure of them. In some of the situations I've been in that's the only way to be."

A lot like Lawrence had been. Decisive. In control. "Is that a prerequisite for being a doctor?"

"Especially for an emergency room one," Max said with no inflection in his voice. He started for the foyer. "Or a doctor who serves on the front lines in a war." At the door he swung around. "Dinner was good. Thanks for asking me. I'll have to return the favor. I'll cook you and your family a dinner some evening."

"That'll be a first."

"What? Someone cooking you dinner?"

"No, a man doing it. My husband couldn't boil water. Once he had some on for tea and forgot about it and the kettle burned a ring into our stove."

"I can assure you I can boil water."

"What made you learn to cook?" Rachel swung the door wider as Max stepped through the threshold on to the porch, the cool, autumn breeze sending her hair dancing about her shoulders like a marionette.

"I started out because I like to eat good food, and there wasn't anyone else to cook for me except myself. Soon I realized I would relax and totally forget about my worries when I did."

"You've never been married?"

His mouth firmed into a straight, tight line. "Once for a few years. A long time ago. It didn't work out."

He might as well have said, "And the subject isn't up for discussion," which only aroused her curiosity. "I'm sorry," she murmured before she really thought what she was saying.

"Why?"

"Marriage can be a good thing. I was married for thirteen wonderful years to a kind man. I hate to see when others don't get to have what I did." It was a once-in-a-lifetime experience. She immediately thought of her mother and her marriage to Rachel's dad. She could still remember the yelling the day her father had stomped away from the house and never come back. Maybe she should try to fix Mom up with Kevin. He was a nice man who could make her happy, feel loved. For that matter, maybe there was someone she could think of to set Max up with a date.

"From what I saw it isn't all it's cracked up to be."

"You just didn't find the right person." There was Carrie Peterson. She might be a good match for Max. No, she worked thirteen-hour days.

"That's all right. I'm not looking. See you tomorrow." He grinned, tipped his head and left.

She closed the door and leaned back against it. Maybe Anne would be right for Max. Heading back to the den, Rachel frowned. No, Anne loved to flirt but didn't want to get serious about any man.

She'd sleep on it and take a look at some of the women she knew at church. Surely there was someone who would be perfect for him.

But by Sunday afternoon as she crossed the street to Max's house, Rachel had nixed every woman she'd come up with. Jordan might want to play matchmaker, even Granny, but she didn't. She would be his friend, help him get acclimated to Tallgrass, but he would have to take care of his own dates.

He answered his door within a few seconds. "You're a sight for sore eyes. I didn't realize I had so many possessions. I didn't have much in the army and I've only been out two years." Stepping to the side, he waved her into his house. "I'm working in the den."

When she entered the room slightly behind him, she came to a stop. Stacked cartons surrounded what little furniture there was—a couch, a lounger and two end tables. "What are in these boxes?"

"Books. Did I tell you I love books?"

"No. Medical ones?"

"Some. That's how I would escape in my off hours

on base. I would read everything I could get my hands on." He gestured toward the built-in bookcases on three walls. "Those are one reason I bought the house."

"You think these boxes of books will all go on those shelves."

"No. I'll have to get more and put them in my office. I'm turning one of the bedrooms into an office."

Rachel put her hand on her hip and slowly rotated in a full circle to take in the work before them. "I'm glad Taylor is going to come over and help when she gets home from the youth group outing."

"Taylor's coming over?"

When she faced him, his expression went blank, but she had caught the surprise in his eyes. "She wanted to. I think she's trying to make up for being rude yesterday. If it's not okay, I can tell her no."

"No. No, I could use all the hands I can get." Turning away from her, he swept his arm across his body. "As you can see."

"Okay, then let's get started. Is there any type of order you want them in?"

He stroked his chin. "Mmm. I guess medical books need to go into my office. The rest in here."

"By genres? Authors? How?"

A teasing glint entered his gaze. "Were you a librarian?"

"We won't go that far and use the Dewey Decimal System. But we could start by separating the fiction from nonfiction, then you can decide."

"Sounds good to me." The smile that started in his eyes spread to encompass his whole face.

And Rachel responded to it, a warmth enveloping her—almost as if he'd wrapped his arms around her. There should be a warning put on that expression. Maybe she could open a window and get some fresh air in here. She slid her gaze to a box nearby. "I'll start with this one. Fiction on that side of the room—" she pointed toward the far wall "—and nonfiction over here."

As he delved into one carton next to him, Max said, "I may have to rethink keeping every book I get."

"There'll come a time you'll run out of space." She lifted up a thick volume on the history of ancient Greece. The book below that one was an equally long text on the history of Rome. Then another on medieval Europe. "I know if Taylor ever needs some research books, you're the person to come to."

"What can I say? I love history."

"You sound like my nephew. I wish Taylor loved to learn like Nicholas."

"What does she like to do?" Max carried a stack of books to the fiction side.

"Oh, let's see. Boys. Fashion. Video games. And occasionally writing. She is constantly writing in a journal. I gave her one after her father died, and she's gone through five."

"A lot of kids hate to write."

"That's about the only thing she likes. Maybe one day she'll be an author of one of the books you collect."

"If she gets a book published, I'll find a special place to put it on my shelf."

Listening to the sincerity in his tone, Rachel caught his gaze. The room separated them, but suddenly she felt as though they stood inches apart. Her pulse rate picked up speed. "That's sweet, especially after how she behaved the past few days."

He raised a shoulder. "She's a teenager."

Tearing her look from him, she dug into the bottom of her first box. "That's no excuse, and she knows it."

Five minutes later when the doorbell rang, Rachel set her armful of books on the floor. "I'll get it. It's Taylor, and I want to make sure she's on her best behavior."

"Sure."

She hurried toward the door, afraid in Taylor's impatience she would press the bell again. Nothing happened fast enough for her daughter.

When Rachel pulled the door open, her daughter marched inside. "Are we gonna be here long?"

"All afternoon."

"That long!"

"What's going on? Why did you offer to help then? Moving isn't a job that's done in half an hour."

Taylor scanned the foyer then stepped a few feet closer to Rachel. "Someone's got to chaperone you two."

Chapter Four

Rachel's eyes widened. "Taylor! Surely I didn't hear you right."

She shrugged. "Well, for an old man he's not bad-looking. And I noticed you like him."

"As a friend, hon." Touching her wedding ring, Rachel twirled it around her finger. "Men and women can be friends. He's new to town and doesn't know anyone."

Taylor snorted. "If you say so." She started for the den. "What do ya need me to do?"

Snagging her daughter's arm, Rachel stopped Taylor's forward motion. "I don't want you to stay if you aren't going to behave. There's a lot to do, and I don't have time to put up with your drama."

Taylor crunched her mouth into a pucker and thought for a good minute. "Sure." Then she yanked her arm from Rachel's grasp and plodded toward the room.

Reinforcing herself with a deep breath, Rachel entered quickly behind her daughter, praying that a war hadn't already been launched.

Taylor stood in the middle of the mountain of boxes. "These are all books?"

"Yep. I like to read." Max stuffed his hands in his front jeans pocket, a hint of uncertainty in his eyes.

"Wow, you sure do. I only read what I'm forced to at school."

Before her daughter declared how much she hated to read, Rachel moved toward her and tapped the top of a box. "We're separating the books into fiction and nonfiction." She pointed to the respective areas of the room to place them.

"What if I don't know?" Taylor's eyebrows slashed down.

"I'll tell you." Max took the carton across from Taylor. "I just appreciate any help I can get."

"Mom, you should have asked Sam and Will. They love to tear into boxes."

Rachel laughed. "And double our workload? No, Nana is doing her part watching those two little munchkins. I think she's taking them for some ice cream."

"Ice cream? I love ice cream." Taylor pouted, looking out the window at the front yard.

"It just so happens I do, too. And since I do, that's one of the things I have on hand. When we take a break, I can fix you all a fudge sundae, double dip," Max said.

Taylor's eyes grew round. "You will? That's my favorite."

From that moment on what tension had been in the room dissipated. Her daughter even giggled at some of the titles of Max's books, especially the medical ones. Rachel relaxed, bent over and dug into the bottom of the carton for the last volume.

When she straightened, Max's gaze ensnared hers for a long, few seconds before she dragged it away, staring at the book in her hand and not really seeing its title. Instead, she latched on to the ring on her left hand, the light gleaming off its platinum surface as though reminding her she'd had the one love of her life. Lawrence had been a good husband and provider. It was so hard to raise three children by herself. It took her full attention. She certainly didn't have time for anything else in her life.

And why was she even thinking about that? She spun toward the stack of nonfiction books and laid her text on the nearest one.

"Mom, I even know that *To Kill a Mockingbird* is fiction."

Rachel glanced down at the hardback. "Oh. Sorry. I was thinking about something else." A wave of heat tinged her cheeks, and she crossed the room to the correct pile.

What was wrong with her?

"Look at this stash!" With huge eyes Taylor scanned the sauces, nuts, cherries, whipped cream and several choices of ice cream as she stepped up next to Max at the kitchen counter.

He chuckled. "I did say I loved ice cream. Do you know what your mom wants?"

"Nothing."

"You're kidding. What person doesn't like ice cream?"

"Not any I know. What do you want me to do?"

He slanted a look at his daughter, not a foot from him. "Just enjoy building your sundae."

"Is a triple scoop okay?"

"If you can eat it, go for it. I've certainly indulged before. Actually, I have some every night before going to bed."

"You do? You aren't fat." Taylor's eyes grew even rounder. "I mean, I didn't…" She fixed her stare on the carton of double-fudge ice cream and began scooping some out.

"I have to exercise to work off that gratification, but it's worth every hour I do. As I'm sweating off the pounds, I'm imagining what flavor I'll choose that evening."

Taylor giggled. "I don't have to exercise. I've always been able to eat just about anything."

"Yeah, well, I used to be able to do that then midlife hit."

"So I have that to look forward to when I get old."

"Ouch!"

Another giggled peppered the air. "You aren't that old."

"Double ouch. I'm suddenly feeling my years. Before long I'll need a cane to walk."

"I'll get Granny to lend hers to you. She refuses to use hers or her walker." Taylor finished filling her large bowl with different varieties of chocolate ice cream.

Max took the scooper from her and delved into the chocolate chip. "She's getting around all right."

"That's Granny. She doesn't let anything get her down."

"That attitude will serve her well."

"I wish I had it more," Taylor muttered while dousing her treat with the rich chocolate sauce.

For a second, Max wasn't sure he heard her correctly but a glimpse of her pensive expression told him otherwise. "There are times I feel the same way."

"You do? You're a doctor. You're smart."

"Does this have something to do with school? What's going on?" *Please tell me. I want to help.* The words *I am your father* were on the tip of his tongue. He wanted to say them so badly, but the time wasn't right. And he couldn't without talking with Rachel first. He owed her that much.

"I just don't like school." She squirted whipped cream on the top of her sundae. "It's boring." Grabbing her bowl, she turned from the counter.

"Do you want a cherry?"

"Nope. That's a fruit. Nothing good for me in this sundae."

"Ah, then you haven't heard chocolate can be good for you."

"It can?" Taylor paused at the door.

He nodded.

"Then why does everyone act like it isn't?"

"Good question. Probably because too much of a good thing is bad."

She cocked her head, looked at him for a moment then laughed. "You sound like my dad."

Her declaration stopped Max in his tracks. His grip on his bowl tightened. He really needed to figure out what he was going to do and soon. He felt as though he were picking his way through a field littered with bombs. "It's the truth."

"Yeah, I know." She swung around and hurried from the room.

If only Alicia had let him know about Taylor all those years ago. He wouldn't be here indecisive, feeling as if any control he had in his life was slipping away. The sound of Rachel's soft voice wafted to him, niggling him with regrets. Any way this worked out, Rachel would be affected perhaps deeper than he because she'd loved and cared for Taylor for thirteen years. What was he doing here?

"Max, I'm going to hold you personally responsible

if Taylor starts climbing the walls because of a sugar overload."

Rachel had materialized in front of him, and he hadn't even heard her approach. Suddenly, she was there—her gentle features arranged in a teasing look that lessened any intended reprimand.

"Oh, Mom, it's just a little ice cream. You could enjoy some if you weren't always on a ridiculous diet."

Red flooded Rachel's face. "I don't diet. I just watch what I eat."

Involuntarily, his gaze roamed down her body. She certainly didn't need to watch her weight. She looked mighty fine the way she was.

Standing at the end of the hallway, with one hand on her hip and the other clutching her bowl, Taylor sighed— loudly. "Whatever." She swept around and flounced back into the den, spooning some of her sundae into her mouth as she went.

Rachel tilted up her chin. "I've changed my mind. I think I'll make myself one." Skirting around him, she crossed the kitchen to the counter and waited for him.

He removed the cartons from the freezer. "Don't let her get to you."

"She isn't. She's right. I usually pass on desserts and stuff like that because I'm worried I'll gain weight. As a teenager I was overweight, and after I lost sixty pounds I promised myself I would never have to do that again." Rachel spooned out two small scoops of vanilla, then squirted caramel on them. "I've never been much of a chocolate person, but I love caramel. Forget the chocolate-dipped bananas or even the cotton candy at the fair. Give me a caramel apple and I'm happy."

He took several bites of his melting sundae, her gaze tethered to his. "I'll have to remember that." The cold dessert slid down his suddenly dry throat. A connection with this woman, all tied up with the girl in the other room, swamped him. He didn't want to feel. He needed to keep a certain amount of emotional distance between them.

While Rachel put the cartons in the freezer again, he ate some more of his sundae and headed for the den, needing the physical separation to pull himself together. He'd worked over the years to keep his feelings under control. It had helped him deal with his difficult job.

When he entered the room, he found Taylor studying a medal with a bronze star dangling from a red ribbon with a blue stripe. "Is this yours?"

"Yes." He watched her face carefully, seeing a play of emotions flash in and out of her features.

"My dad had a Bronze Star, too. He kept it on the wall in his office. He was very proud of it."

Whereas he didn't display his. It brought back too many memories of the war he didn't want to remember or discuss. He hadn't put it away yet, and it had still been on the top of his cluttered desk.

"So you were a soldier?"

"Yeah, in the army."

"My dad was in the air force. Once a year he would get together with some of his buddies. He was supposed to leave to meet them right before he had a heart attack. I'd asked my dad if I could go this time, but…"

Each time she said "dad" a stab of pain pierced his heart. He took a step toward her, not sure what to say.

Tears shone in her eyes. Averting her head, she laid the medal back on the walnut desk. She covered the few feet between them and held out her hand. "I'll take your bowl back to the kitchen."

Numbly, he placed it in her grasp and watched her rush from the room, flying past her mother in the doorway.

Rachel gave him a puzzled look. "What happened?"

Glimpsing the medal, Max fingered it for a second then snatched it up and walked around the desk to put it in the top drawer. Memories of mangled bodies in a building after a bomb explosion took over his thoughts. He shook them away and lifted his gaze to Rachel. "She told me about her father being in the air force."

"Was that the Bronze Star?" Rachel gestured toward the desk.

"Yes. She mentioned her father had one, too."

"Now I understand why she was upset when she left. She used to have her dad tell her about how he got the medal. I imagine he told her at least a hundred times over the years."

"Should I say something to her?"

She shook her head. "I will. I need to put my dish in the kitchen, anyway."

As Rachel left, Max sank back against the still-empty bookshelf behind him. This wasn't going to be easy. Would Taylor even accept him in the end? What would he do if she didn't? The very thought swelled the tightness in his chest until he could hardly breathe.

"I'll handle the food at Granny's reception. You and Mom can do everything else." A few days later, Jordan sat at the table in Rachel's kitchen jotting down the plans for their grandmother's reception in two and a half weeks.

"In other words, I'll do everything else." Rachel eased into the chair across from her sister. "You know Mom is going to be worthless. Throwing parties has never been her forte and she isn't exactly into Granny's marriage."

"Granny doesn't want a fuss."

"Too bad. I want to fuss over her. She's always been there for us. I'm glad she's only moving across the street."

"Speaking of across the street. How did Sunday afternoon go with your new neighbor?"

An image of Max popped into her mind. After Taylor asked about the medal, he'd been quiet. Even her daughter had commented on it when they left his house later. "What do you think about Sarah Johnson?"

"Concerning what?"

"Introducing Max to her."

"Why?" Jordan narrowed her eyes. "Never mind. I know why. You're afraid."

"Of what?" Rachel dropped her gaze from her sister's and stared at the wedding list she'd written.

"Oh, let's see. One, meeting a nice man who interests you. Two, starting to have feelings for him beyond friendship. Three, do I have to say anymore?"

Rachel wanted to deny it. She couldn't. It was true. "He is a nice man. Even Taylor warmed to him some on Sunday."

"And that probably scared you even more."

"No—okay, maybe a little. I think it was the ice cream sundae that got to her."

"The way to a female's heart is through ice cream?"

Rachel chuckled. "Yeah, something like that."

"How's she doing at school this week?"

"I'm not sure. Monday and Tuesday she came home and didn't say a word. I mentioned again about home-schooling, but all she did was stomp off to her room."

"Zachary's sister told me Taylor called Ashley last night to ask about homeschooling."

"She did? She didn't say anything to me." Frowning, Rachel pushed to her feet. "But then why should I be so surprised? We don't talk like we used to. I'm usually the last one to know what's going on with her. Did Ashley say if Taylor was interested in homeschooling?"

"I think she just listened. Didn't say much about how she felt."

The sound of the front door slamming closed jerked Rachel around toward the kitchen entrance. Her heart pounding, she rushed toward the foyer. She glimpsed Taylor stomping up the stairs.

"Taylor, what's wrong? Why are you home from school at eleven?"

Her daughter whirled around at the top. Her bottom lip quavered. She bit her teeth into it as tears filled her eyes.

Rachel ascended a couple of steps. "Honey, what happened?"

Taylor opened her mouth to say something, snapped it closed and spun on her heel. As she fled down the second-floor hallway, her sobs resonated through the house.

"I'm leaving. Go talk to her." Jordan sent her a reassuring look. "Maybe she's ready to talk."

Or not. Rachel hurried up the stairs as her sister left. At Taylor's room she knocked, waited a few seconds and turned the knob. Entering, she found her daughter on her bed, crying, her body shaking from the force of her sorrow. Her legs were curled up against her chest while her back was to Rachel. The painful throb in her chest expanded. Hearing her child so upset tore Rachel up more than if she were the one in distress.

She sat on the bed and laid her hand on Taylor's arm. She stiffened beneath the touch and hunched her shoulders even more. "Taylor, talk to me. Tell me what's going on."

For a long moment her daughter didn't say anything, then she muttered, "I'm the dumbest kid in school."

"What happened?"

"I made the lowest score on the science test on Monday and then today in history. Everyone knows it."

"Did they say anything?"

"No. But they don't have to." Taylor turned to face her. "I saw the pitiful looks I got. I'm not going back to school. Ever."

"You just got up and walked out?"

"Yes, in the middle of class. I want to be home-schooled. It can't be worse than what this year has been like."

"Okay, if you're sure."

A tear rolled down Taylor's cheek. She swiped it away only to have it replaced by another. "Yes. I can't go back."

"Then we'll start tomorrow afternoon. I'll go up to school this afternoon and talk with them. I want to know where you are academically. Tomorrow morning you have an appointment to see Dr. Reynolds." The office had called earlier that morning to say there was a cancellation, and the receptionist moved up her appointment from next week.

"Why?"

"I want to talk to Dr. Reynolds about Attention Deficit Disorder."

Taylor shot up in bed. "You think I have it?"

"I don't know what's going on with you, but something is. You haven't been for a check-up in a while. I want to make sure everything is all right." She reached out to her daughter. "I'm concerned about you. You're always upset and angry."

Taylor shrugged away from Rachel's touch. "I'll be fine now. Ashley told me about homeschooling. I can work at my own pace. I won't feel so lost."

Something in her daughter's expression doubled Rachel's concern. "Yes, you'll be able to, but you'll have to work. Just because you won't be in school doesn't mean I don't expect you to learn everything you need to."

"Whatever." Taylor rolled over and presented her back to Rachel.

She counted to ten, still wasn't calm and headed straight for one hundred. *Lord, I'm going to need lots of patience. I've always thought I had some, but now I don't know if that's true.*

Finishing up with a patient, Max exited the exam room at his new office and nearly ran right into Rachel and Taylor. "Kevin said you and Taylor were coming in this morning. How did the appointment go?"

The smile Rachel gave him warmed his insides. "It went well."

"There's nothing wrong with me," Taylor said, then flounced down the hall.

"That's good." Max watched his daughter disappear through the doorway into the waiting room.

"It will be once we get into a routine. I'm starting homeschooling this afternoon. Kevin diagnosed Taylor with ADHD. He gave me some stuff to read about it. Some tips for teaching her, which I'm very grateful for."

"Have you gotten a chance to read the book I gave you Sunday on ADD?"

"Yes. Good thing I've got support through Helping Hands Homeschooling Group and my sister doing this. I don't think I could do it alone. And Kevin suggested the science class he teaches."

She might not know it, but he would be there to support her, too. "That'll be good. He's already recruited me to teach it the week after next. He's going to a conference."

"Great. I won't have to deal with science then."

"She'll have homework."

"Something my daughter doesn't like to do. We've had battles over it at the kitchen table." She glanced toward the direction of the waiting room. "What was I thinking? How is homeschooling going to be any different?"

"You guys sound like you need something fun to focus on. Tell you what. I'll take you all out to dinner tonight to celebrate the first day. I owe you for helping me on Sunday." He wanted to spend as much time with his daughter as possible.

"Sam and Will, too?"

"Sure." Like a regular family dinner.

"You're a brave soul."

"Are you warning me?"

"Yep, if we don't pick a fast-food restaurant, I don't know how long the boys will last."

He snapped his fingers. "I've got a better idea. I fix a great pizza. Why don't you all come over to my house tonight at say six? You can now walk through the den. My boxes are only confined to the living room."

"Are you sure you're up for this?"

No, but there was no way he would tell her that. He hadn't figured out how to get to know his daughter without being around Rachel. And if he got to know her well, how was he going to be able to tell her he was

Taylor's biological father and he'd come to Tallgrass to be a parent to his only child? If he wanted to be in Taylor's life, he didn't have a choice.

"Yes, or I wouldn't have offered," he finally said as he began walking toward the waiting room with Rachel.

When she got to the entrance, a frown crinkled her brow. "Where's Taylor?" She took several more steps and made a slow circle.

"Maybe she went to the car?" Although his voice was calm, his gut knotted.

"Yeah, that's probably it. I'd better go before she decides to walk home."

"I'll come with you. If she isn't out there, I'll help you look for her."

Rachel made her way toward the office door. "I don't want to take you from your patients."

"You aren't. We're shutting down for lunch."

They rode the elevator to the first floor in silence. The whole way Max couldn't dismiss the thought that Taylor was hurting and upset. Many children with ADHD did impulsive things with no thought to the consequences. Had she?

"My car's in the second row." Rachel pointed toward her Lexus SUV.

As they neared, Max noticed the vehicle was empty. Glancing around, he saw no sign of Taylor. The tightness in his stomach hardened into a rock.

Chapter Five

Her heartbeat thundering in her ears, Rachel checked the car's interior to make sure Taylor wasn't hiding. Its emptiness mocked her. She'd handled this all wrong. Lately, that was all she seemed to be doing with her daughter—taking one step forward and two or three backward.

"Where would she go when she's upset?" Max asked, concern edging his voice and expression. He made a slow circle to scan the parking lot.

Rachel did likewise. The glare of the noonday sun glinted off the vehicles' surfaces and hurt her eyes. "Maybe a friend's. But since they're in school, I guess that's out. Maybe the arcade. Maybe to Mom's. She's at work, but Granny will be there."

"Call your grandmother while we go to the arcade. I'll drive." Max led her to a red Mustang she'd seen in his driveway.

After she settled in the passenger seat, she dug her cell out of her purse and called Granny. She let the phone ring until the answering machine came on. She left a short message about Taylor being gone.

"Where's this arcade?" Max started his vehicle and backed out of his parking space.

"Three streets over on Sheridan near First. In the middle of the block."

"Does she go to the arcade a lot?"

"She's been there a few times. She likes to play video games. Some of the teens hang out there. It's a safe environment thankfully. But dark and noisy. I don't know how she can stay there for more than a few minutes." The tremor in her voice leaked into her body. She clasped her hands together to still their shaking. She wanted her little girl back—the one who wasn't moody. The one she could talk to.

"We'll find her."

As he turned down Sheridan, Rachel peered toward him. "I appreciate your help. I'm sure she's okay, but I'm at a loss what to do about Taylor anymore. I'm hoping homeschooling will help, but what if it doesn't?"

"Then you'll find another answer."

The tightness in his voice caused her to study the hard set to his expression. He caught her look and some of the tension eased from his features. "My brother went through a similar time with his son."

"What happened?"

Max parked in front of the arcade. "He ran with the wrong crowd. Did some stupid, even some dangerous things. The last one, joyriding, woke my nephew up, but not before Brendan had gone through the wringer."

"How old was he?"

"Fourteen. He's seventeen now and doing much better."

Would it get that bad with Taylor? The thought sent terror through her. As she climbed from the Mustang, she gripped the door frame to steady herself. She felt so alone in that moment.

Max appeared at her side. "She'll be okay. My brother refused to acknowledge anything was happening until the situation got bad. You know Taylor is having problems and are willing to find a solution. And you've got my help. I may not be a parent, but I've worked with children, teens. Some very troubled." He held out his hand.

She fit hers in his, and for a brief moment she didn't feel so alone. Walking toward the entrance, she thought about Max coming into her life at just the right time when she needed someone who understood what was going on with Taylor. *Thank You, Lord, for sending him to Tallgrass.*

After inspecting every dark corner, the music and bells and dings on the machines booming through the air, Rachel emerged outside in the sunlight, relishing the quieter atmosphere on a street several blocks from the main thoroughfare through the town. "I really didn't think she would be here, but I needed to check it out since she was caught sneaking in here during school last Friday."

"Where do you want to go next?"

"Home. I want to see if she is at Mom's. Sometimes Granny doesn't pick up the phone because she doesn't move fast. She actually told me once she doesn't understand the need of us youngsters—me included—needing to be available 24/7 with their cell phones. She wanted to know when I had any downtime."

"She's got a good point."

"My grandmother usually does."

"I'm still going to find a way to wheedle that fudge recipe out of her."

Rachel tried to suppress her chuckle but couldn't. "I wish you the best with that one. She would be a great spy. She doesn't give anything away she doesn't want to."

Max pulled onto their street. "Do you want to check your house or your mother's first?"

"Mine. Maybe she came home. I can always hope."

"Yeah, hope is important."

The way he said that last sentence alerted her that there was more behind his statement than the mere words. She locked gazes with Max as he brought his Mustang to a stop in her driveway. "If it wasn't for the Lord and my family, these past few years would have been so much worse than they were. And believe me, it hasn't been easy holding a family together when your husband dies suddenly."

"I'm glad you had something."

She slid from the front seat and stood, staring at him over the top of his car. "It sounds like you didn't."

"Let's just say I haven't found the Lord there for me when I needed Him." He pivoted and strode toward her house.

She quickly followed, wanting to pursue the subject, but the tense set of his shoulders and clenched hands forbade it. Music blared behind the closed front door. "She's here or at least she was. When she turns the music up loud like that, she's really upset. She usually uses her iPod otherwise."

Inside the foyer, the vibrations blasted Rachel. "I'll go up and see if she wants to talk. Thanks for helping."

"I'll be here when you come down."

"You don't have to be. You'll need something to eat before you go back to work."

"My next appointment isn't until one-thirty. It won't hurt me to go without lunch. You might need someone to talk to, and besides, someone will have to take you back to get your car."

"Oh, I forgot." Which she was discovering she did a lot around her new neighbor. As she hurried up the stairs, she felt the heat of his look on her, and instead of sending her into a panic, she responded to it with a quickened heartbeat.

Rachel didn't bother to knock on Taylor's door this time because the music was so loud she wouldn't hear, anyway. When she entered the bedroom, Taylor sat on her bed cross-legged with Rachel's laptop, studying the screen intently. She marched over to the CD player and switched it off.

Blessedly, silence ruled for a few seconds before her daughter jerked her head up and glared at her. "Mom, I was listening to that."

"And the whole neighborhood. Use your iPod."

Taylor returned her gaze to the computer.

"What are you doing?" Rachel crossed to the bed and stared down at the screen.

"Reading about ADHD."

"And?"

Taylor lifted her head and looked directly at Rachel. "This sounds like me. I do a lot of these things. I don't like to sit for long. I have a hard time paying attention. I..." Wonder replaced any hostility from earlier in her voice. "They say here there's help for it."

Rachel sat beside Taylor. "That's what I wanted to tell you. There are things we can do to help you cope with it. I'm reading about it and learning everything I can so I can do that."

"I need to do that, too. I want to understand what's wrong with me."

"Hon, everyone has strengths and weaknesses. I do.

You do. Your brothers. We'll take your strengths and build on them and work to deal with your weaknesses. We're in this together. You aren't alone."

Taylor threw herself into Rachel's arms and hugged her so tightly for a second she couldn't get a good breath.

When she pulled back, Rachel asked, "Are you okay?"

Taylor nodded as she turned back to the computer. "Can I read some more about it?"

"That sounds great. I have to go pick up my car at the doctor's office."

"How did you get here?"

"Max brought me. We went looking for you. He didn't want me to drive since I was so worried about you."

"I'm sorry." Her gaze focused on the Web site about ADHD.

"After I get back, we'll have lunch and talk some more. Okay? We need to get started on homeschooling today."

"Fine." Taylor agreed but there was no enthusiasm in her voice.

Rachel waited a moment to see if Taylor would say anything else or ask another question. When she didn't, Rachel left, feeling for the first time in a long while a ray of hope even if her daughter wasn't excited about schoolwork.

When she descended the staircase, Max sat on the bottom step, his elbows perched on his thighs, his hands clasped loosely between his legs. He glanced over his shoulders, a question in his eyes.

"She's reading about ADHD on the Internet. She's better. I think she's actually a little relieved to find there's a name to what she has been privately struggling with, especially the past few years."

He shoved to his feet and rotated toward her. A smile ignited his eyes and enveloped his whole face. "Good. I'm so glad to hear that."

His expression, as though they shared something, nestled a warm feeling deep in her heart. "I told her I was leaving for a little while to pick up my car. She wanted to read more about what she'd found. Which is great because Taylor doesn't read if she can help it."

Max strolled toward the front door and stepped out on to the porch. "She struggles with reading?"

"Yeah. I intend to do a program to help her read better. Dr. Baker gave me a suggestion, and I ordered it. One of the reasons she has difficulty is because it takes her a long time to read. She would often give up before she finished a selection for school. At least at home, I'll be able to adjust the instruction with that in mind."

At his car he pulled the passenger-side door open for her. "That sounds like a good strategy. A lot of subjects hinge on the ability to read."

"I'm counting on it to help my daughter. I just hope I'm doing the right thing. Jordan struggled with that issue, too, and Nicholas is doing great with homeschooling."

Max rounded the front of his Mustang and climbed in behind the steering wheel. "What Taylor was doing wasn't working. Maybe this will."

"That's what I'm hoping. Lately, I've felt helpless where Taylor is concerned. Nothing I'm doing is getting through."

As he backed out of the driveway, his look brushed over her—as though he'd physically touched her. Her throbbing pulse coursed through her. His clean, fresh scent surrounded her, vividly making her aware of the man sitting only a foot from her.

"From what I've seen, you're a great mother. You care for your children and want what's best whatever that is. You're willing to try homeschooling to help your daughter. That'll be a time commitment for you."

"Before I married Lawrence, I took a few classes toward being a teacher. I always wanted to be one. I guess I'll find out how well I would have been. If it works for Taylor, I'll consider doing it for Will and Sam. They'll be starting kindergarten next year." She grinned. "But I appreciate your vote of confidence."

"I'm pretty good at science. If you need any help there, I can help."

"Thanks. I may take you up on that once we get into the classes with Kevin."

"Call me if you get frustrated."

"I'm good at math and English. I think I've got that covered. Jordan and her sister-in-law do a history class together. They said Taylor can join them."

"Sounds like you've given this a lot of thought and got everything covered."

She drew in a deep, composing breath. "Then why do I feel like I'm out of my comfort zone?"

"Because you are," he said with a laugh. "You aren't a teacher and have never homeschooled so it will be scary at first."

As he drove into a parking space near where her Lexus was, she couldn't shake the feeling this man understood her. The loneliness she'd felt these past few years after Lawrence died dimmed some.

She put her hand on her handle, twisted toward him and said, "Thank you. You don't know how much I appreciate the help today."

"You're welcome." He switched off his engine while directing his full attention to her.

Looking into his eyes, the color of sun-kissed grass, she swallowed hard, a link between them strengthened in that moment. When she first met Lawrence, she'd connected with him. The realization she was experiencing the same sensation excited her and yet scared her, too. As she got out of the car and closed the car door, she peered down at the wedding ring on her hand. Skirting the back of his Mustang, she twirled the band on her finger, part of her feeling guilty as though her thoughts betrayed her husband's memory.

"See you this evening," Max said when she passed him in the parking lot.

She gave him a smile, full of gratitude and something else. Interest? Her last expression stayed in Max's mind all the way up to his office. Seeing the struggles that Rachel was going through with Taylor sobered him. Rachel was a good mother. How could he do a better job? And what was going to happen when Taylor discovered he was her biological father? Would she hate him? The same could be said about Rachel. How would she take the news?

When he'd seen both Taylor and Rachel in the office hallway earlier, he hadn't planned on asking her and the children to dinner. But the invitation had tumbled from his mouth before he could stop it. Rachel's nearness affected him in ways that he hadn't anticipated. Alicia had never been that caring or warm. He'd had little of that in his marriage and being around Rachel illustrated what he had missed.

"Mom, do I have to? We've been working for three straight hours. I've got to have a break." Taylor threw down her pencil on the paper and pushed back her chair.

"We stop when you have finished that row of problems. You only have three more to go." Rachel moved closer to her daughter and pointed toward the pre-algebra on the workbook page. "You had a break before you started this math. We've only been working on it for twenty minutes."

"Don't Will and Sam need you or something?"

"No, I just checked on them, and they're playing in Sam's room."

Slouching against the kitchen table, her elbow on its top, Taylor settled her chin in her palm. "I can't work with you standing over me."

Rachel thought of a Bible verse on patience and repeated it several times in her mind as she took the seat next to her daughter. "Is this better?"

"No. You don't have to watch everything I do. I'm not a baby."

"Fine." Rachel rose. "I've got something I wanted to give you. I'll go get it while you finish the problems."

When she halted at the entrance into the kitchen, she looked back to see Taylor staring out the window. Rachel bit her lower lip to keep from saying something. Homeschooling was going to take a long adjustment for her daughter.

So far, in the first afternoon, Taylor had managed to avoid as much work as she could whine her way out of or come up with a reason not to do it. She got a drink—four times. Went to the restroom more than she ever had before in the span of three hours. Got caught texting several friends. And moaned about how hungry she was even after having a large ham and Swiss sandwich with a mound of chips only an hour before.

With a deep sigh, Rachel retrieved the journal she'd bought for Taylor, checked on her sons, now in the den, and returned to the kitchen to find her daughter still staring at the window, dusk quickly evolving into darkness. "Hon, we've been invited to Max's for pizza tonight. If you can't get your work done, I'll have to call him and tell him we can't come."

"Pizza," Taylor murmured her favorite food and pulled her attention from the window to focus on the sheet in front of her. She sat up straighter and hunched over the paper, pencil in hand.

Rachel hung back, not wanting to disturb Taylor as she worked first one problem then the next and finally the last equation.

Taylor slammed down the pencil. "Done."

Rachel covered the area between them and placed the journal down in front of her daughter while Rachel took the math and checked the rest of the answers. "This is good. The only thing you need to do is refigure the last step in the first problem." She put it down on the table and pointed to the one she was talking about.

"Just mark it wrong and give me the grade."

"No, I'm not grading you. If you get something wrong, you'll fix it until it's right. We don't move ahead until you understand what we're working on."

"Oh, please, you expect me to do everything right. I can't."

"You will and can. Remember, you'll determine how fast we move."

Taylor huffed and erased the numbers, then redid it. "There. Okay?"

"Great. I knew you could do it."

"What's that?" Taylor pointed to the journal.

"I got you another journal. Before we start our lessons each day, I want you to write in this your thoughts about anything that happened the day before. You can show it to me or not. That will be your choice."

"If you don't grade it, what good is it?"

"I want you to write for the pure joy of writing."

"There's nothing joyful about writing or reading."

"I thought you liked to write. You've gone through five journals in two years."

"I don't like anything having to do with school."

"I hope I can change your mind." *If my patience lasts that long.*

Taylor rolled her eyes. "I don't have to now, do I?"

"No, you can start tomorrow morning."

"When do we go to dinner?"

Checking her watch, Rachel started for the den and the noise of arguing. "In half an hour."

Taylor passed her in the hall, hurrying toward the stairs. Rachel increased her pace as a crash reverberated down the corridor. She appeared in the den at the exact moment Will and Sam were playing tug-of-war with a book. Her gaze fell upon a chair on its side, and she inhaled a relieved breath.

"Boys, stop it."

"I had this first." Will yanked on the book and a couple of pages ripped off in his hand.

"I did."

Rachel stepped between them, snatched the book before it was completely ruined, and wondered what she had gotten herself into. How was she going to keep Taylor focused on her schoolwork and be a referee for her two sons at the same time?

"This is the best pizza I've ever had." Taylor polished off her fourth slice and collapsed back against her chair. "I'm stuffed."

Will reached for the last piece in the center of Rachel's kitchen table. "I claim this."

"No, I want it." Sam managed to get his hand on the pizza a second after his brother and a tug-of-war began again.

"Stop right now." Rachel schooled her voice into the calmest level possible under the circumstances of a war being played between the twins—a war that had spilled over from earlier in the den through the whole dinner with poor Max sitting and taking it all in quietly. Neither boy would let go of the piece. "Put it back on the plate."

"But I claimed it first." Will glared at Sam.

"I'm still hungry." Sam narrowed his eyes to slits and sent daggers toward Will. "I'm not letting go until he does."

While the two were staring each other down, Rachel rose slightly from her seat and snatched the slice from both of them. They turned their looks on her. "Obviously, it's time for bed. Go get ready, and I'll come up to tuck you in."

"I'm not sleepy." Sam glanced at Will. "This is all your fault."

"No, it's yours."

"Now, and I don't want to hear another word from either one of you."

The twins stood, pouts descending. They spun around and raced for the door.

"Haven't you two forgotten your manners? What do you say to Dr. Connors for fixing the pizza?"

Near the kitchen entrance, each jockeying for being the first through the doorway, both boys came to an abrupt halt and slowly turned, slanting a look toward the other to make sure he did the same thing.

"Thanks," Will and Sam said together, then whirled around and bumped shoulders while hurrying out of the room.

The pounding of their footsteps up the stairs echoed through the house. The slamming of their bedroom doors quickly followed. Then silence.

"Now you see why I asked you to come over here to eat. I had a feeling something like this would happen." Rachel leaned back and relaxed for the first time, her stomach muscles releasing their tension. "I'm sorry you had to hear that. They've been at each other's throat all day. Hopefully, tomorrow will be better."

"It kind of reminds me of my brother and me when we fought." Max sat at the head of the table where Lawrence had. The sight of Max there startled her at first, but as so much that had occurred in the past two years, it was something she got used to quickly. Lawrence wasn't coming back, and she had to move on. Make a new life.

"If no one's gonna eat that last piece, then I will." Taylor grabbed the slice, part of it falling apart from the tug-of-war. That didn't stop her from taking a big bite of it.

"I thought you were stuffed," Max said with a chuckle.

"I just needed to wait a few minutes. Can't let pizza go to waste."

"I'm glad you liked it." A pleased expression eased the tired lines on his face.

"One of my friends' dads cooks a lot, too. But my dad never did except to barbecue steaks every once and a while."

"I like good food, and I got tired of going out to eat

to get it. But you should have seen my first attempts. Uneatable is a kind description."

"My aunt Jordan and Granny are great cooks."

Rachel straightened. "I think my daughter is saying I need more lessons."

"Let's just say your sewing is better than your cooking." Giggling, Taylor finished off the last bit of pizza.

"Okay, so I didn't inherit the cooking gene from Granny." Rising, Rachel picked up her dishes. "Now that we're through—"

Taylor bolted to her feet. "I'm going to research some more on ADHD. Thanks for the pizza."

Before Rachel could blink, her daughter was halfway across the kitchen.

"I'll help you clean up." Max gathered up the plates near him.

"You don't have to. I'll do it later. You've done enough cooking dinner. And I agree with my kids. The pizzas were delicious." Max had prepared three different kinds—a supreme, one that reminded her of a Greek dish, and a pepperoni, her boys' favorite—and she'd tasted each one.

"We can talk while we clean up." Max set the plates in the sink. "How did it go today with Taylor?"

"Basically, we went over what she found concerning ADHD. We discussed it, and she feels better now that she understands it some. Other than that all we accomplished was half a page of math, and that subject is one of her better ones. I don't even want to think about tomorrow when we start in the reading program."

"Any change won't be easy for Taylor. I have found kids with ADHD don't like change." Max cleared the rest of the table while Rachel began filling the dishwasher.

"Actually, not many children do. For that matter, I

don't. I know this will be hard, especially at first, but I'm determined to help Taylor. Tomorrow I'll begin to set up our routine and try to stick to it as much as possible. I think Taylor needs that right now more than anything. The literature I've read stresses that."

Max came to stand next to her and help her load the dishwasher. "Don't forget yourself in all this. What do you need?"

Chapter Six

The second Max uttered that question he wanted to take it back. He had no business getting too involved in Rachel's personal life because in the end, that wasn't going to change the fact he wanted to be in his daughter's life.

"What do I want?" Rachel paused in handing him a plate and thought a moment. "I want my children to be happy and safe. I'm not really worried about Sam and Will. But I am about Taylor. Lawrence's death was hard on her. I know a little about what she's going through."

"Your dad died when you were her age?"

"As a child, I might have said worse than that. He walked out and left my mom. Cut off all ties. She struggled to take care of us and to get over the emotional abandonment. I was nearly thirteen at the time and tried to help her as much as possible, but I didn't understand why he would leave and not let us know where he was. I still don't. How can a parent turn his back on his own child?" She held up her hand. "I know it happens all the time, but it doesn't make it right." The past etched her voice in pain.

And touched him with memories of his own past with

Alicia. She'd taken his right to be a father away from him—had given up her own child because she didn't want to be bothered with raising her. This was a woman he'd loved, married. How was it possible he was so far off base with what Alicia was really like? Ever since he'd discovered the existence of Taylor he'd questioned his judgment. He'd made a terrible mistake believing in Alicia that caused him to lose years with his daughter. What if he did something equally terrible and lost Taylor for good?

"No, it doesn't make it right." He closed the dishwasher. "You don't know where your father is?"

"No, and I don't want to know anymore. I gave up dreaming he would come back to Jordan and me long ago. That kind of abandonment leaves its mark on a child."

"But Taylor's dad didn't purposefully abandon her." He wouldn't have if he'd known about her.

"Oh, I know—" she averted her head "—but being left behind still hurts." A raw ache resonated through Rachel's words.

Drawing him to her, he settled his hand on her shoulder, the muscles beneath his palm taut. He placed his finger under her chin and rotated her toward him. Her eyes glittered with unshed tears. She swallowed hard and dropped her eyelids to veil her expression. "Rejection is hard no matter who does it."

She shuddered beneath his touch. "Who hurt you?"

"My ex-wife. She left me while I was overseas serving my country. I didn't even get a 'Dear John' letter. I got a notice through her lawyer that she was divorcing me." *Tell her. Get it over with. Ask to be in Taylor's life and get out of here.*

Then Rachel reestablished visual contact with him, and a connection sprang up between them—had from the very beginning. Two people who knew what it was like to be rejected by a loved one. He didn't know what to do anymore. He didn't want to hurt Rachel, and yet Taylor was his daughter.

She cupped his face. "I'm so sorry to hear that. It's bad enough being separated from your loved ones while serving. You certainly don't need to worry about something like that. Did you ever talk to her?"

"No, I lost touch with her until her younger sister called me a few months ago and told me she died. A freak accident."

"Sometimes you just have to put your past behind you and let go of the heartache."

Her fingers against his skin branded him, riveting him to her. The gentle look in her expression lured him even closer until there were only inches between them. Her lavender fragrance reminded him of a flower garden his mother used to have where he and his brother played cops and robbers among the bushes. The memory heightened his desire for a family. Taylor was his family. He couldn't walk away. What kind of father would he be then?

The direction his thoughts was going sobered him. He pulled away and put several feet between them. Taking deep breaths, he calmed the quick beating of his heart that her nearness produced. "Have you put your past behind you?" His look latched on to her wedding ring.

"I'm trying and mostly I have." She closed her right hand over her left one.

Everything was happening too fast. He needed to step back and slow things down. He needed to think carefully through what he was going to do or rather when he was going to tell her about Taylor. Before the holidays? After them?

Indecision blanketed him in a cold sweat. He didn't

like feeling this way. "I'd better go. Tomorrow will be a long day for you and me."

"Maybe we should compare notes tomorrow night and see who had the longest day?" Her light tone sounded forced as though she, too, was gathering her composure after that little exchange.

"Do you ever go for a run or a walk?"

"Exercise?" she asked, as though it was unheard-of.

"Yep, so you can eat tons of ice cream."

"Not often. Usually the boys want to go, too, and then it doesn't really serve its purpose."

"How about we all go tomorrow? Get Taylor, too."

Rachel laughed. "Taylor? She wouldn't be caught dead going for a walk with her family."

"Have you asked her?"

"Well, no, but my daughter tries to find excuses not to do stuff with us."

"Ask. She may surprise you. Tell her we can end up at the ice cream store near the park. My treat. Since it gets dark early we'll go at four. Are you game?" There was a part of him listening to him persuade her to go with him that couldn't believe he was speaking. What about slowing down did he not understand? And yet, he felt as if time was running out for him. Taylor was already thirteen. She'd be a grown-up young lady soon.

"Sure. I'll have Sam and Will ride their bikes. They're begging me to take off the training wheels, but I don't know if they're ready yet. All I see is one accident after another."

"Sounds good to me—the walk, not the accidents. I'll see you out front at four." A few more paces back but still facing Rachel, he hesitated. He'd enjoyed himself and didn't want to leave yet.

"Mom, Will and Sam are having a pillow fight," Taylor

shouted from the second floor, wrenching Rachel's gaze from his.

"I think this is round three. I need to go." Rachel rushed toward the hallway. On the staircase, she paused and added, "See you tomorrow. Are you sure you're ready for my sons going with us?"

Was he? Doubt nibbled at his mind. "Sure." Especially if his daughter was there. That was the reason for all this. "Bye."

A crash jerked Rachel around, and she continued her trek up to the second floor while Max opened the front door and left. Descending the steps to the sidewalk, he rotated around and glanced up at the bedroom above the porch. Rachel came over and started to close the drapes, caught him looking and waved.

He returned it, a smile appearing and chasing away the frown that had been on her face. Her warm expression twisted his gut, reminding him of the reason he was in Tallgrass. He really didn't know how this could turn out good. Someone was going to lose—Taylor. Rachel. Himself. Would he and Rachel end up like the twins in a tug-of-war over Taylor? The picture didn't set well and churned his stomach even more.

The more he was around Taylor the more he realized he needed his daughter to know him before he broke the news who he was. That was the only way it would work. Tomorrow afternoon would give him a chance to move forward on his plan.

Max sat at the table with Rachel late the next day at Frozen Delights while her two sons were climbing on the play equipment in the enclosed playground. He'd been disappointed to find that Taylor had gone to spend the night at a friend's house. He'd been looking forward to getting to know his daughter better. In the back of his mind he felt a clock ticking down toward disaster.

"How was homeschooling today?" Max took a lick of his German chocolate cake ice cream.

Rachel swung her gaze from her twins to Max. "Difficult. I couldn't get her to focus longer than ten or fifteen minutes. I'm looking for some good instructional computer games to help keep her attention. By the afternoon, I decided to work fifteen minutes then take a short break. The afternoon went better than the morning."

"Take what she is interested in the most and use that to help teach her." He remembered it had helped him when he was learning to read.

Rachel ate a spoonful of her peppermint ice cream. "She loves playing games, especially video ones, so I'm going to use that. I've looked online and ordered some, but I'm going to a teacher's supply store in Tulsa when I go for the quilting competition the first of December. I'm going to make it a family outing."

"I've heard good things about Tulsa." He bit into the cone, nearing the last of his treat.

"Yeah, it's a pretty city. The kids enjoy going. You're welcome to come, too. In the afternoon my quilt will be displayed at the museum. There's a small reception for the quilters and family at five."

"You'll have to show me one of your quilts."

"I'm finishing up the one going to the museum. I'll show you." A blush colored her face a pleasing tint.

"Having your work displayed in a museum sounds like quite an honor to me."

Her cheeks reddened even more. "Yes, I was surprised when I was included. The quilts are from different places and people in a five-state region." She took another bite of ice cream.

He watched her slide the spoon between her lips. He couldn't pull his attention from her mouth, perfectly formed. Suddenly, he put a halt to his thoughts. The situation was complicated enough without thinking about how it would feel to kiss her. "What time are you leaving?" He fixed his gaze on hers.

"I was going in the afternoon, but if the weather is nice, we could go earlier and go to the Tulsa Zoo in the morning. They decorate for Christmas, and I think the kids would enjoy it. I could use it with Taylor. One of her favorite animals is an elephant. The Tulsa Zoo has an elephant demonstration she's wanted to go to. She's talked about joining the Friends of Tulsa Zoo Elephants. This might be a good time to do it."

"I'll see if I can rearrange my appointments to take the day off. Kevin will be back in the office so it shouldn't be a problem."

"Great. While I'm on a roll, Granny wanted me to ask you to her wedding and reception next Saturday."

"She did?"

"You made quite an impression on my grandmother last weekend. She told me it would give you another chance at badgering her about the fudge recipe."

Max laughed. "I'll wear her down. You just wait and see."

"Granny loves a good challenge."

"Like her granddaughter?"

A smile quirked the corners of Rachel's mouth—one he needed to quit staring out. "Yes, it's in the genes. Now if I could just get Taylor to look at learning as a challenge."

"Learning is a challenge. For some more than others. It wasn't easy for me, but one day I decided if I wanted to be a doctor I had to take control and learn in spite of my problems."

"You had problems?"

"A few with reading as a child. But as you can see, I love to read now, and I didn't let it stop me."

"It'd be great if you could share that with Taylor some time. Would you?"

"If you think it would help." The idea appealed to him. He hadn't told many people about his struggles to learn to read, but if it would help his daughter, he would.

"If she hears how you overcame your struggles and went on to be a doctor, that should help her. There was a time she wanted to be a doctor just like her daddy. The past few years she hasn't said anything about that. All she tells me is she's undecided. I think she's giving up on that dream because she's been having trouble with science. That used to be all she talked about."

"Then I'll find a time to talk to her." When Rachel had talked about Taylor's dad, his chest had constricted until now he had to force deep breaths into his lungs.

"Did you say something about teaching for Kevin next week?"

"Yeah."

"You could after the class. I could come a little late and give you some time."

"How about I bring her home? The class is at the end of the day, and I'll talk to her on the ride home. Okay?"

"Perfect." She scanned the playground for her two sons. "This has been nice even if I had to walk a mile to get some ice cream."

"And now we have to walk back. Are you ready?" Beyond the glass enclosure Max noticed the sun sinking behind the trees, dusk settling over the landscape. "Good thing there are sidewalks all the way. We might not make it back before dark."

"That won't bother Will or Sam. They'll think it's an adventure, riding their bikes after dark."

"If you want, I'll help you with teaching them to ride without their training wheels. I was home on leave when my brother taught his son. I think I've got the hang of how to do it."

"Yeah, there's a lot of running along beside the bike until they get their balance. Or at least that's what Lawrence did for Taylor."

Max rose, turning away from Rachel so she wouldn't see anything written on his face. But that was another experience he'd missed as a father. He hadn't been there when she'd learned to walk, talk. Her first day of school. Another man got to do what he should have done.

Rachel says to put the pain of the past behind me. But how? Alicia robbed me of so much.

At her wedding reception on Saturday, Granny held up her hand, palm outward. "You aren't gonna get the fudge recipe."

"Are you sure there isn't something I could do for you to change your mind?" Max's green eyes gleamed with mischief.

"There's only one way—being a family member." Dressed in a cream-colored silk suit, Rachel's grandmother looked pointedly from Max to Rachel standing next to him. Granny grinned and winked.

Rachel wished the floor in the rec hall at Tallgrass Community Church would open up and swallow her. Granny wasn't known for being subtle, and this definitely was one of those times she might as well shout her intent to everyone in the rec hall. "Granny, you haven't told us where you two are going on your honeymoon."

She snorted. "Honeymoon? We live on a fixed income. We don't have that kind of money, nor do I want to waste it on something like that."

"Can I treat you to at least a weekend at the Tallgrass Inn by the lake?"

"No, child. I'd rather you give that money you'd pay for the weekend to some cause that needs it. Besides, I have my own plans for this weekend." Her grin grew, her eyes sparkling. "Doug and I will be just fine. Speaking of Doug, where is that young man? Ah, I see him over by Eileen. I'd better go rescue him. My daughter is probably giving him the riot act right about now." Granny shuffled toward the opposite side of the large room, filled with friends and family.

"Your grandmother tells it like it is."

"That's my granny." The heat of her embarrassment still tinged Rachel's cheeks.

Max surveyed the rec hall. "So, this is your church. How long have you attended?"

"All my life."

"Your kids have grown up here, too?"

"Yep. Taylor especially loves coming. She's part of the youth group, which is very active. We've talked about her joining the choir because she loves to sing. I wouldn't be surprised if she does soon because she loves Christmas music."

"Is her faith important to Taylor?"

"A lot of things have changed in the past few years especially since my husband died, but that hasn't thankfully."

"You don't feel like the Lord has let you down." A

shadow darkened his eyes as though a memory gripped him—an unpleasant one.

"No, on the contrary. I don't know what I would have done if I didn't have Him in my life. He helped me through some tough times."

"I'm glad He helped you." The way he'd said the sentence highlighted his disillusionment with God.

His tone saddened Rachel. "But He didn't help you?"

"It was hard to keep my faith when I saw so much suffering and pain in the war. There were some guys I pleaded with the Lord to ease their hurt because I felt helpless to do it." His voice dropped a level, a thick huskiness in it.

"What happened to those soldiers?" She moved closer to hear his answer in the din around them.

"Some died. Some returned to the States and had to face a long recovery."

"But that doesn't mean God wasn't there with them. The believers who died went home to the Lord like Lawrence did. The others were never alone unless they chose to be. The Lord doesn't guarantee a pain-free life, only that He'll be with you every step of the way, holding you up."

"I didn't ask anything for myself."

"Maybe you should. Maybe you should start a personal dialogue with God."

Max turned away. "Your sister is waving at you."

"Oh, I think it's time for Granny and Doug to cut the cake. I have to help serve it."

"Save me a chocolate piece."

"That's all there is. My granny might be as bad as you about chocolate."

"If you're comparing me to your grandmother, then I'll take that as a compliment. She's special."

Rachel searched for Granny in the crowd. "Yeah, she is."

Ten minutes later, after her grandmother had cut the cake, then stuffed some into Doug's mouth, laughter besieging both her and her husband, Rachel stood next to Jordan serving the dessert while her sister sliced the masterpiece she'd spent hours making and decorating. When Max approached the table behind Zachary and his attention honed in on Rachel, her hand shook as she stretched it out toward him. His fingers grazed her, and for the life of her she didn't know how she didn't drop the plate with the chocolate cake and thick white icing on it.

"Thanks. This will satisfy my sweet tooth for the time being." Max sidled down the line to grab some punch and finger sandwiches. He popped a cucumber and cream cheese one into his mouth.

She couldn't pull her attention away from that mouth. What would it be like if he kissed her? The second she thought that she wanted to snatch it back. She had no business thinking about that. Didn't she just declare a few weeks ago she wasn't interested in getting involved with a man?

"Rachel, quit daydreaming. You're falling behind in your duties." Jordan presented the next woman in line a plate since Rachel couldn't seem to pull her gaze away from Max.

Her younger sister nudged her with an elbow in the side, dragging Rachel back to the here and now although she enjoyed watching Max move away and join Taylor, Eileen and Kevin at a table.

"You have it bad, sis," Jordan whispered into her ear.

"I don't know what you're talking about." But as if she had no control over her reactions—and she was beginning to feel that was the case—she blushed, the heat flaming her cheeks.

"Sure, you just keep denying you're interested in a certain new neighbor."

"Shh. Someone will hear and think you know what you're talking about."

Jordan went back to slicing the rest of the cake while guests passed by for their treat. But Rachel couldn't help thinking about what her sister said. Her gaze slipped occasionally toward Max. Once, he threw back his head and laughed. Taylor joined him, the sound beautiful to Rachel's ears. Then Kevin leaned forward and said something to them and their laughter increased. Even her mother relaxed and smiled.

When the last of the cake was served, Rachel headed for the table where Max was. There was one seat beside him, and she eased into it.

"This is the best cake," Max said about eating the last bite of his piece. "Can we have seconds?"

Rachel peered at what was left. "Yes, please do. Otherwise, we'll have to take it home."

"I wouldn't want you to have to do that," Max said with a chuckle and stood.

Her mother angled toward Kevin next to her. "Now that you've had a partner for two weeks, how's it working out?"

"I'd forgotten the benefits of working with a partner. Next week I'm going to a conference and he's even taking over my homeschooling class. I did everything I could to warn him." Kevin threw a glance at Taylor. "Very sharp students who ask a lot of questions. How'd you like your first week?"

"It was fine. Mom's helping me with the homework."

Rachel had spent hours working with Taylor, especially on reading the material. The large, more difficult vocabulary gave her daughter trouble, but they were using flash cards to help with that.

"Good, Taylor, but if there's anything you need me to explain, stay after and ask me. I don't have any patients after the class so I have the time."

"I can't believe you take the time to do the class. This parent is very appreciative you do."

"It was that or tell my sister no. Nancy is very persuasive."

Rachel was glad that Dr. Nancy Baker had talked her brother into teaching a science course because for the first time in a long while Taylor hadn't put up a fight to learn the subject.

Max returned to the table, bringing two plates. He set the second one out in the middle close to Taylor. "In case anyone else wants another piece." He looked right at her daughter.

Taylor beamed and slid the cake toward herself. "Thanks."

"Us chocolate lovers have to stick together."

"Granny would agree to that." Taylor cut into the slice and brought it to her mouth, her eyes closing for a few seconds. "Aunt Jordan does make the best."

"Can I have everyone's attention? I need all unmarried women gathered around me." Granny waved her arms toward herself, standing in front of the serving table where the remnants of the three-tiered cake, nearly gone, remained.

Rachel stayed in her chair, watching the other ladies weave their way through the crowd toward her grandmother.

When there were twenty women surrounding Granny, she parted the group and looked right at Rachel. "That includes Rachel and Eileen. You two aren't married. Hop to it. I don't have all day. Every second counts for me."

Rachel groaned. She didn't want to get up in front of everyone to vie for the bride's bouquet. When she approached Granny, she said, "This is for ladies who have never been married."

"Yeah, Mom." Eileen leaned around Rachel. "I'm too old for this."

"Only in your mind. Lighten up. Enjoy."

Granny shuffled back to the front of the group of women. "Okay, line up behind me and I'll toss my flowers to the next person who will be getting married."

Rachel tried to sidle away, but Granny sent her a sharp look so she inched back to the edge of the crowd. Her grandmother turned around, brought her hand with the bouquet in it down, then raised it. Right before she released the flowers, she peeked over her shoulders and aimed it right at Rachel. She hadn't intended to go for the bouquet, but it hit her square in the chest and on reflex she grabbed it before it fell to the floor.

A cheer went up around her.

Her mother patted her on her back. "Glad it was you, not me. I was afraid Granny had an agenda."

Yeah, one to embarrass me. The fragrance of the roses wafted to Rachel. Their scent brought back memories of her own wedding and marriage. She'd had a good one, so why was she afraid to get involved with a man? By the time she'd married Lawrence, she'd known him for two years. He'd been a mentor then a friend before she'd ever had any deeper feelings. She'd known Lawrence would never leave her willingly—like her father had.

Granny slowly made her way to Rachel. "My aim is

as good as ever. Some things peter out with age but for me not that."

"Nor your interfering, Granny. I'm not on the market." Rachel tried to put a stern tone to her voice, but when she looked into her grandmother's pleased, happy expression, she couldn't.

"I hope you got the hint. I like our new neighbor. And besides, he's determined to get that fudge recipe and the only way that poor man can is to marry into the family. We wouldn't want to disappoint him, would we?" Then her grandmother sauntered toward Doug.

And now Granny lived even closer to Max—right next door rather than down the street.

Chapter Seven

"I enjoyed today. I never knew there were that many germs on common things." Taylor fastened her seat belt in Max's Mustang after science class the following week.

"Most of the germs are harmless. Some people think we are too obsessed with cleanliness, that children don't build up their immunities like we used to." Max pulled out of his parking space at his office.

"What do you think?"

"I'm usually a middle-of-the-road kind of guy. Not extreme on either side of the argument. That's why we're studying germs this week and learning when and where to be more careful. Especially with flu season here."

"It was weird but fun."

"Weird?"

"I've never seen a germ under a microscope. I never thought of it as moving around."

"Yeah, they are a life-form. If you need any help on your presentation about Louis Pasteur, I can help."

"That probably wouldn't be fair since you're the teacher. I wouldn't want anyone to accuse me of being a teacher's pet. Believe me, I've never been one."

"But I'm only your teacher this week and the presentation isn't until next week."

"Nicholas offered to help me. He could if Mom's busy. My brothers can be a handful at times."

Something in her voice made Max slant a look at her. "What's wrong?"

"I shouldn't have to get a child years younger than me to help me. I don't care if he's a genius. It should be the other way around."

"Nicholas is unusual. You shouldn't compare yourself to anyone. If you do your best, then you're doing what you should. That's all you should expect."

"But it's hard. I want to do good, but…"

Scenes from his own childhood paraded across his thought—the struggles, the self-berating. "But reading doesn't come easy."

"No. It takes me forever to read a chapter and then I forget what I've read."

"You may not want to hear it, but what you need to do is practice even more. The more I read as a child the better I got."

"But you're a doctor. Smart."

Max pulled into his driveway, switched off his engine, then shifted toward Taylor, hoping he could do something to help his daughter. "It wasn't always like that. When I was in elementary school I had a lot of trouble with reading. I couldn't seem to learn using the phonetics method, which is what they taught at my school. I even went to a reading clinic. I was so embarrassed. I wouldn't tell any of my friends."

Her green eyes, so like his, widened. "What did you do?"

"I got mad. First at myself. Then at my parents. Then I just got mad and decided I wasn't going to let it win. To tell you the truth, I didn't even know what it was. Now I do."

"What?"

"An auditory processing problem. I don't hear sounds like others do so that means I have to work extra hard to compensate."

"You do?"

"Yeah, having a learning disability, which is what they call it today, doesn't mean you aren't smart. It does mean you might have to do things a little different from others, from how it's normally done at school. But you have the chance to do that with your homeschooling."

"How so?" Puzzlement greeted his look, her forehead puckered.

"Like I said, practice more than most have to. If you can't learn reading by the sounds, then you may have to memorize what others don't have to. I know it's a lot of extra work, but the end result is worth it."

She twisted her mouth into a thoughtful expression. "You really had trouble?"

"I failed reading in third grade. My fourth-grade teacher brought me to tears once. That's when I got mad and decided I had to do something to change the situation."

"And you didn't have any problems after that?"

"I didn't say that. I still struggled when I came up against something I wasn't familiar with. Like science. In junior high I hated it. By the time I got to high school, I began to like science, especially how everything worked. The human body is remarkable. My favorite class became anatomy. It was the hardest A I made in high school."

"Hmm." Taylor pushed open her door and grabbed her book bag.

Max climbed from the car and peered at her over

the top of it. Her features visible still in the dim light of dusk, he saw something that gave him hope he'd helped her. She was thinking about what he'd said. That was a start.

"Thanks for bringing me home."

"Anytime."

She jogged across the street toward her house. Max watched her make it safely to her porch before heading toward his own home. When he let himself inside, the emptiness that suddenly surrounded him as he moved through the rooms to the kitchen produced a hollow feeling in the pit of his stomach.

He wanted more than a few minutes here and there with his daughter.

"Mom, do I hafta do this? Will and Sam don't." Taylor shook the rake she held toward her little brothers watching Max remove their training wheels from their bikes. "They get to have fun with Max while I work."

"I'm raking, too." Rachel stood in the middle of a blanket of leaves, her attention straying toward her sons with Max.

"Max was supposed to help me with my presentation for science today." The corners of Taylor's mouth dipped down in a pout. "He probably forgot."

"He hasn't forgotten. He told me he planned to later this afternoon."

"I can't believe I have to do school on Saturday." Taylor attacked the dead leaves scattered around her.

"We've talked about this. We set the time for home-schooling. And besides, today you're doing homework like you would if you were in regular school."

"I'm first," Will shouted in the driveway.

"No, I am. I'm the oldest." Sam got on his bicycle and nearly fell to the concrete.

Rachel dropped her rake and marched toward the twins. She had been afraid this would happen. They had become quite competitive with each other lately. Why was her whole family falling apart?

Before she had a chance to say anything, Max stepped between the boys. "Will asked first, so he'll go first." He looked pointedly at Sam, who hung his head.

Rachel slowed her pace.

"You two will get the same amount of practice. No one will have more than the other. Tomorrow I'll start with Sam if we need to work some more." Max lifted his head and locked gazes with Rachel.

She came to a stop a few feet from the trio. Her heartbeat reacted to the twinkling expression in his eyes, tapping a fast staccato against her chest. "Do you need any help?" The breathless quality to her voice spoke of his effect on her. She couldn't deny she was attracted to him any longer.

"Nah. Will, Sam and I understand each other. Don't we?" He didn't take his attention from Rachel.

And she didn't from him. But her sons piped in an enthusiastic yes. "Good. I know they appreciate you helping them." She finally tore her look from him and took in both boys.

They nodded, both gripping the handlebars of their bikes. They were miniature Lawrences with blond hair, dark brown eyes and clefts in their chins, reminding her of her husband.

"Good." She whirled around and strode toward her daughter. Her wedding band gleamed in the sunlight, mocking her recent thoughts about Max.

Her children would never understand her interest in

another man besides their father. They had been through so much in the past few years she didn't want to disrupt their lives anymore, especially Taylor. She had to think of them, not herself, now.

For the next hour she raked leaves alongside her daughter while Max helped Will and Sam ride without their training wheels. Once Will crashed and she started for him, but before she'd gotten three steps, her son jumped up, dusted off his jeans and hopped back on. Max held on to the back of the seat a little longer than previously before he let go. Will rode on the sidewalk all the way down to his grandmother's house, five away.

He came to a stop, twisted around on the seat, beaming from ear to ear. "I did it! I did it!"

Max gave him a high five then followed Will back toward her.

"Are you all ready for some hot chocolate?" Rachel asked as she filled the last bag with leaves.

Taylor carried it to the curb. "Yes."

"Great. We'll do the backyard another time." Rachel picked up both rakes and followed her boys to the open garage to put up their bikes. "Max, would you like some hot chocolate?"

He tapped his finger against his chin. "Let me see. I love chocolate in any form. I wonder what my answer will be." An impish gleam danced in his eyes.

She playfully slapped him against his arm. "I'm assuming no. Am I right?"

"I'll turn down chocolate when pigs learn to fly."

"Pigs can't fly," Sam chimed in as he opened the door into the house.

"It's just a saying sort of like the man in the moon. Not possible." Max tousled Sam's hair and trailed him inside.

"But a man was on the moon. Pigs flying I don't see unless they ride in an airplane." Taylor pressed her lips together to contain a giggle that burst forth anyway.

Max nodded his head. "You've got a point. I suppose anything is possible."

"Yeah, through the Lord," his daughter said, shrugging out of her coat and placing it on the hook by the door.

Max blinked, his eyes growing wide. He slowly smiled. "Then what we talked about a few days ago is possible."

Taylor paused, throwing a pensive look over her shoulder at Max. "I suppose."

Will pulled Taylor's hand. "I want to show you what I built this morning."

"Yeah, I helped him." Sam ran out of the room behind his siblings.

"No, you didn't. You almost caused it to topple." Will blocked Sam from passing him.

"I was helping."

While Rachel's kids continued to argue, Max watched them disappear down the hall toward the den, then shifted toward her. "I can go referee if you want."

"Nah, I'll step in when I hear shouting. Taylor will handle it. She's good with them."

"Yeah, I noticed." He moved closer to her. "Do you need any help with the hot chocolate?"

"Like the fudge recipe, I work until I master this. I boil water then stir in a package of mix. I think I can handle it."

One of his eyebrows rose. "A package mix?"

"Ah, don't tell me you fix it from scratch." She switched on the burner to heat water.

"Then I won't."

She crossed her arms. "Don't say a word to my kids about that, or they'll start insisting I do. Quilting is my hobby, not cooking."

He chuckled. "And you wouldn't catch me holding a sewing needle. My lips are sealed. Not a word about my special recipe."

"If not, I'll send the kids over every time they want hot chocolate, which in winter is about every day." Trying her best not to stare at those lips he was talking about, she rummaged through the pantry until she found her mix.

"I'll keep that in mind. But one day I'll have to prepare it for you all." Max lounged against the counter dangerously close to her. "Speaking of your quilting, when do I get to see the one you're working on?"

As she set five mugs on a tray, she slid a look sideways. She could reach out and graze her fingertips over those lips so easily. Instead, she balled her hands and kept them down. "After I deliver these to the kids. My newest one is in the den. This one is for Jordan and her family."

"Sounds like a labor of love."

"All of mine are, but this one is special. It will be their first Christmas together as a family. In fact, this Thanksgiving will be a first, too. We're having a huge gathering at the ranch this year." She finished preparing the hot chocolate and lifted the tray. "If you don't have plans for Thanksgiving, why don't you come with us to Jordan's?"

"Other than cooking my turkey for one, no, I don't have plans."

"No one should be by themselves at the holidays. I hope you'll come."

"Are you sure? Don't you need to ask your sister?"

"Ha! She'd be mad if I didn't ask you. Kevin is coming. Since his wife died, he's come every year."

When she mentioned Kevin's wife, Max's forehead crinkled, his eyes darkening. What happened with Max and his wife? She sensed whatever it was left a mark on him—one that went deep into his soul.

"If you're sure, I'd love to. I don't relish spending Thanksgiving by myself." A hint of vulnerability threaded his words.

She made her way toward the den, wanting to help him. He'd been hurt, and it sounded as if he hadn't healed yet. "You can count yourself part of the family this holiday."

Inside the room, Rachel set the tray on the gaming table. Immediately her children flocked to her and grabbed the nearest mug. She gave one to Max and took the last cup while her sons went back to their tower they had started this morning.

"Taylor, do you want me to help you with your presentation?" Max took a sip of his drink.

"Yeah, I'll get the laptop and show you what I've got so far. Pasteur came up with the germ theory." Taylor put her mug on the tray and hurried toward the hall.

A faraway look came into his eyes as he observed Taylor leaving. "Where's that quilt?" he finally asked, returning his attention to Rachel.

Had he wanted children with his wife? A wistful expression often captured his face when he was with her kids. "You know I never asked if you have children?"

"A girl."

"Where is she?"

"With a good family." He spotted the quilt lying over a lounge chair by the window and stepped toward it. "Is this what you're working on?"

A shutter descended over his features but not before she glimpsed the pain in his eyes he couldn't mask fast enough. The subject was taboo. Whatever happened with his wife most likely involved his daughter and a great deal of hurt. Her heart went out to him. She knew how important her children were to her. Maybe one day he would share it with her and possibly then his burden that was eating at him.

She held up the cream, green and red quilt with panels of Christmas objects—a star, tree, stocking, wreath.

"This is beautiful. Does your sister know?" Although his expression was neutral, his voice quavered.

"No, and my kids know they can't say a word. I want to surprise her."

"She will be. You've put a lot of work into this."

"Ready, Max?" Taylor appeared at the doorway, hugging her laptop against her chest. "Mom, can we work in the kitchen?"

"Sure, hon."

Taylor spun on her heel and made her way down the hall.

Max started toward the entrance into the den.

Rachel grasped his arm. "Thank you for helping her. She's already getting tired of me always helping. We're still working out a routine that works for both of us. Not easy when she doesn't want to stay still."

"It's the least I could do," he murmured and left.

Rachel wondered about his last sentence until the sound of a collision of blocks with the hardwood floor crashed through the air. They flew everywhere. The next thing she knew her sons were wrestling. She rushed over to them and hauled Sam off Will.

Tears of anger streaked down Sam's cheeks. "He knocked it over on purpose."

"Did not."

"Did, too."

"I don't care at the moment. What I do care about is that this mess is cleaned up, and you two take a time-out from each other for the rest of the day." Rachel released Sam, staring from him to Will. "Now."

While she watched her twins gather all the blocks, she thought about Max and his daughter. What happened to her? Why didn't he have her since his wife died? She hoped one day he would confide in her because she had the feeling it weighed on him.

"You didn't have to bring anything to eat. You're my guest." Rachel slipped from her SUV and rounded the back to pop the trunk. The scent of Max's sweet potato casserole drifted to her. "But I'm glad you ignored what I said about a dish. This smells delicious."

"It's my own creation, a couple of recipes altered and combined." Max grasped the pan and lifted it out. "What did you bring?"

"Fudge and a broccoli-cauliflower salad." She slammed the trunk down and started for Zachary's sister's house.

"A woman after my own heart."

Her stomach flip-flopped at the casual remark he made. Worse, it didn't send her into a panic, which left her baffled. What was happening to her? Common sense told her not to complicate her life. But her heart wasn't listening. She never rushed into anything and these sudden feelings concerning Max unnerved her.

"There are a lot of cars. Who's going to be here?" Max climbed the porch steps.

"Besides Jordan, Zachary and Nicholas there are Zachary's sister Becca and her husband, Paul. They have three children, Mike, Cal and Ashley. Ashley and Taylor are friends. Zachary's parents are here visiting and then my mom, Granny, Doug and Kevin."

"A crowd."

"Yep."

"My family is small. We never had more than eight people and that was in a good year."

Rachel put her hand on the doorknob. "Are you ready for the onslaught?"

"Most Thanksgivings lately I've been working, so this will be a change."

"I'm hoping a good one. But I'll warn you it'll probably be loud. With seven kids running around, it would be nearly impossible for it not to be."

"Does Zachary's sister hand out earplugs at the door?" Max asked over the noise coming from the living room as Rachel stepped through the threshold.

"You know that's not a bad idea. We periodically escape outside for a reprieve. Maybe I should have warned you."

He smiled, lines fanning out from the corners of his eyes. "I'll be all right. I wonder how Taylor handles all this stimuli."

"She gets a bit hyper, but she isn't the only one. The kids feed off each other. We'll take it for a while then banish them to play outside."

"Are you two gonna just stand in the door and chat or come inside?" Jordan approached them, reaching out for Max's pan. "I can take that and put it in the kitchen for you. Go into the den. That's where the men fled to."

"Which way?" Max sidestepped while Nicholas and Mike raced past them out on to the porch, Jordan's son bumping into Max's arm.

"Slow down," Jordan said as Becca's son Cal and both

twins quickly followed the other two guys. "It's gonna be a long day. Thankfully, it's nice outside."

"The den's in back, down the hall and to the left." Rachel nodded her head in the direction of the den.

Max made his way toward the hallway. Ashley and Taylor hurried from the room, almost bowling him over. He threw a wide-eyed look back at her before he disappeared into the den while the girls hurried toward the porch.

Rachel stopped in the foyer and shouted after the teens. "Taylor and Ashley, will you two keep an eye on Will and Sam?"

"Yeah, Mom. We're going down to the barn to look at the animals."

"Does Zachary know?"

"Yep. It's okay. He suggested it." Taylor vanished outside.

Quiet engulfed Rachel for a moment until loud voices, each child trying to outdo the others, resounded in the air.

"At least they aren't arguing." Jordan headed for the kitchen.

Rachel remembered the overwhelmed expression momentarily on Max's face. She chuckled to herself, wondering if today would be a shock to his system.

Max strolled down to the barn with Rachel to round up the children for the Thanksgiving dinner. "Zachary has a nice setup here."

"Yeah, we come out here riding sometimes. Taylor especially likes to. That's how she got to know Ashley better. They both belong to the youth group at church but didn't have much to do with each other until my sister reconnected with Zachary."

"Reconnected?"

"They were high school sweethearts. Both left Tallgrass and went their separate ways. They married last month."

"Zachary and Nicholas sure have hit it off. I know step situations can be hard sometimes."

"Zachary is Nicholas's father, but he didn't know until Jordan came back to Tallgrass in August."

"Nicholas is, what, eight or nine?"

"Ten and yes, my sister kept it a secret for almost eleven years. Something I didn't condone."

Max paused at the corral. "And Zachary forgave her?"

Nodding, Rachel observed the horses in the field next to the barn, settling her arms on top of a slat of wood on the fence. "There was a time she, and frankly I, didn't feel that Zachary would. To say the least, he wasn't thrilled with her for keeping it from him."

An omen of things to come? Max now knew he couldn't keep who he was from Rachel much longer. He might have to keep quiet a while longer with Taylor, but not Rachel. Ideally, he would like to get to know them, especially Taylor, better before he dropped the bombshell on them. The thought of what he needed to do settled like a molten rock in the pit of his stomach.

"But the Lord wants us to forgive, and Zachary saw the wisdom in that."

"Sometimes that's easier said than done." A picture of Alicia materialized in his mind. He shook the image away.

"True. I had to struggle to forgive my father for abandoning us when I was a teenager."

Max slanted a look at her, his arm next to hers on the fence. "And there are no regrets about forgiving him?"

"No, it's freeing to let go of that anger. I won't tell you his leaving us didn't color my view of life. When I met Lawrence, I had a hard time trusting him or any man. I was so afraid he'd walk out just like my dad did. It was Lawrence who showed me the importance of letting it go."

Rachel made it sound easy. He didn't think he could let go of his anger toward Alicia. She robbed him of so much out of spite because she didn't get what she'd wanted—the kind of life she'd dreamed of as a doctor's wife. Was his inability to forgive the reason he avoided church? Everything had changed when Alicia had divorced him. Slowly, he'd let go of his faith, especially when he'd seen so much death around him while serving in the army in war-torn areas.

Rachel pushed off the fence and walked toward the barn. "We'd better go get the kids. It'll take time to get them back to the house and washed up." Coming to a stop in the entrance, she surveyed the children all going in different directions. "Tell me why we volunteered to do this."

"Beats me."

Sam chased Will while Taylor patted a horse that was hanging its head over the bottom half of a stall door. Nicholas was practicing roping a post, followed by Cal and Mike. Ashley emerged from the tack room, her jeans dusty, hay stuck in her long hair.

"Kids, it's time for dinner," Rachel said in a level above normal.

Nothing.

"Here, let me." Max put two fingers in his mouth and blew a loud shrill whistle.

The children halted and turned toward him.

"Dinner is on."

All at once they dropped what they were doing and charged toward the entrance—the one he and Rachel stood in the middle of. He grabbed Rachel's arm and yanked her toward the side with him.

As they raced out of the barn, Rachel yelled, "Wash up before you sit down to eat."

"Do you think they heard?"

Grinning, she said, "Beats me," then peered down at his hand still on her arm.

She was so near it seemed so natural to lift his hand and cup her face, pull her even closer. The fragrance of lavender shrouded him in sensations he wanted to deny. He was attracted to Rachel. Her lips, full with a sheen of lipgloss on them, beckoned him to sample them. He shouldn't. Too dangerous.

The temptation overwhelmed him, and he dragged her against him, settling his mouth over hers. Tasting her spearmint-flavored toothpaste. Relishing the feel of her in his arms, the soft strands of her hair as his fingers delved into it. She shivered and cuddled closer within the circle of his embrace. The gentle whoosh of air from her parted lips and the glazed look in her eyes when he leaned back attested to her reaction to his kiss.

As much as he knew it wasn't a smart move, he wouldn't have taken it back. He'd wanted to kiss her for days. Now the mystery was over. He could move on. And yet, when his gaze zeroed in on her mouth where his had been seconds before, he realized he was dreaming if he thought he could forget and proceed as though nothing had happened between them.

"We'd better get up to the house or there won't be anything left," Rachel murmured, a shaky huskiness in her voice.

"Are you kidding? I saw that feast before we left. It could feed an army."

"Not with seven ravenous kids."

"Oh, good point. Then let's get moving." Max grasped her hand and set a fast pace toward Becca's front porch.

When they entered, chaos ruled with everyone talking, finding his or her seats. Will and Sam ran through the group to get to the same chair. They began tugging it between them until Granny clamped her hand down on Will's shoulder while Doug took Sam's.

"Behave, you two, or into the kitchen with both of you."

The boys' eyes grew round as the dinner plates. "Yes, ma'am."

Rachel marched over to the twins with her hand on her hip. "I want you all at different ends of the table. One wrong move and you'll be banished to the kitchen for the rest of the meal."

"Can we take our food?" Sam claimed the chair they'd been fighting over by sliding into it before Will.

"No. If you have time to cause trouble, then you must not be too hungry."

Will glared at his brother and trudged to the opposite side of the children's long table and plopped down.

Max came up behind Rachel. "You're a regular drill sergeant."

"You have to be when you have two active boys the same age who are best friends at times and enemies at other times. Thankfully, best friends wins out usually. It's just been lately I don't know what's gotten into them."

"You'll figure it out. You're a good mother." It would

be so much easier if she wasn't, but Rachel loved and cared for her children.

He helped Rachel into her chair, scooting it into the table, then he took the place next to her. Everyone finally settled down. The second after Zachary blessed the food, Ashley and Taylor reached for the dish nearest them, scooped out a good portion then passed it to the person beside them.

"Granny, how's married life?" Ashley asked right before shoveling in a mouthful of corn bread dressing.

Rachel's grandmother blushed a nice bright red shade and swiveled her attention to Doug. "The best. I recommend it for everyone." She passed her gaze over first Rachel then Eileen before flittering to Kevin and lastly Max.

Max felt his face get hot with embarrassment. Marriage wasn't for him. His one experience was enough to make him shy away from the institution. "Marriage certainly has its appeal for some people, but not everyone."

"Have you tried it, young man?"

Rachel dropped her fork on her plate, the clang ringing in the air. "Granny!"

Max cut his roasted turkey. "Yes. I have." Then he forked a piece of meat and brought it to his mouth, keeping his look glued on Granny.

The room grew quiet. Max stared at Rachel's grandmother, and she stared back. A twinkle sparked her eyes. "There's nothing like having someone to share your happiness or your troubles with. Friends and family are certainly nice, but a partner is so much better."

"I'm sure that's true for you." *But not me.* Max clamped his mouth down so he didn't utter the last part of the sentence. He'd enjoyed the kiss with Rachel. In fact, his response to it only reconfirmed he needed to shore up his defenses. He would end up hurt if there were any emotional ties between them, especially in light of who he was.

The reason he was here was for Taylor. And only Taylor.

But as the rest of the meal progressed, the good-natured teasing and conversation around him tugged at him. What would have happened if he and Alicia hadn't divorced and they'd raised Taylor? He would have had the family he'd wanted.

"Who made this sweet potato casserole?" Granny asked, dishing up a second helping.

"I did." Max relaxed back, stuffed after eating too much turkey, dressing, homemade cranberry sauce, fresh green beans and biscuits.

"Delicious," Rachel's grandmother said with a ripple of agreements going around the table. "I'd like to get the recipe from you."

"I wish I could, but it's a family secret." Max slipped a look at Rachel, who could hardly contain her laugh. He winked at her.

Granny snorted. "And you would gladly give it to me if I traded my fudge one for it?"

"You and I see eye to eye." He grinned.

"I think I'll take some home with me. We'll see if I can't figure this out." Granny dug into the helping of the sweet potato casserole on her plate.

Leaning toward him, Rachel whispered, "I think she's thrown down the gauntlet."

"Maybe I could get that fudge analyzed. Do you know any labs that might do that around here?" Max asked in a serious voice, then he winked at Rachel again.

Rachel looked at him a few seconds then burst out laughing.

"What's so funny, Mom?" Taylor took some more of the sweet potato casserole, too.

"The battle for the recipes between Granny and Max. He has been wanting her fudge one."

"Oh, that one you've been trying to teach me."

Max sat forward. "She has? We'll have to talk later, Taylor."

His daughter giggled. "I know never to make Granny mad."

"Isn't she such a good kid?" Rachel's grandmother finished her meal and lounged back, a satisfied smile on her face.

Yeah, Taylor is. And I want to be part of her life. The more he was around his daughter, the more he knew that. If only he could do that without anyone getting hurt.

Chapter Eight

Today, Rachel would be driving to Tulsa. The thought she wouldn't be alone brought joy to her. Not just her children would be with her, but also Max. Staring at herself in the mirror, she held up one outfit after another, trying to decide what to wear. Since they were going to the Tulsa Zoo as well as the Philbrook Museum for the reception and quilting display, she needed something practical and casual that could be dressed up for later in the day.

Finally, she held up a long flowing skirt with the fall colors. She had brown boots she could wear to the zoo and heels for the reception. As she laid her clothes for the trip on her bed, she zoomed in on her wedding ring, the sun's rays streaming into the bedroom highlighting it.

Instantly, the picture of her and Max kissing on Thanksgiving flashed into her mind—with all the sensations that kiss produced in her. Her heart thumping against her chest. The swirling in her stomach as if a whirlwind had raged inside her. And in a way it had.

She cared about Max. Could see him as more than a friend if she totally let go. She loved Lawrence—always would—but she was lonely. Spending this past month with Max made her realize she did want more.

Sinking on to her bed, Rachel twisted the ring around on her finger. *Am I ready? Lord, how do I know?*

She stared at the platinum band with a diamond solitaire. Her teeth dug into her bottom lip. The churning in her stomach settled down. In that moment, she sensed the Lord surrounding her in calmness.

She gripped the ring and slid it off her finger for the first time in years. Pushing herself to her feet, she crossed to her jewelry box and set it inside. She would never know if she didn't take the risk.

"Mom, you got first place for your quilt." Taylor waved toward Rachel's creation draping on the wall at the Philbrook Museum.

Rachel stopped a few feet into the large room where the quilts were on display. Across the expanse, hers—a large decorated Christmas tree on a cream background bordered in forest green—hung in the middle with a blue ribbon attached to it.

"It's beautiful. I'm impressed," Max said close to her ear.

A tingle shivered down her length from the brush of his warm breath on her neck. "Thanks. It took me a good part of the summer to do it. It was hard to get in the holiday mood when it was a hundred degrees outside."

"I haven't had the pleasure of a summer in Oklahoma yet, but it can't be worse than the desert where I was stationed some of the time."

"Will you take a picture of me and the children with the quilt?" Rachel dug into her purse and withdrew her digital camera.

"Sure."

She lined up Will on one side of the quilt and Taylor and Sam on the other. Then she stood next to Will. "Smiles." When she saw Taylor hold up two fingers behind Sam's head, she added, "This one is a serious picture."

"Then we can't smile," Will said, squirming next to her.

"I mean no funny business on this one then we can get crazy in the next one."

After Max took the photo, he handed the camera to a lady watching them. "Will you take a picture of us?" When she agreed, he hurried to Taylor's side. "I have to get in on the funny one."

"Okay, this time nothing serious." Rachel swung Will into her arms.

Max pulled out a pair of sunglasses while Taylor stretched out on the floor beneath the quilt and Sam sat on her.

"Ready." The older woman put the camera up to her face.

Max made a funny face while Rachel tickled Will and he giggled.

After the lady snapped the picture, she brought the camera to Max and said, "You have a beautiful family."

For a second, a frown skittered across his expression before he fixed a smile on his face and said, "Thanks, but I'm just a friend."

Just a friend. What if it were more? Rachel had removed her wedding ring. Did he notice or care? Before she'd dated Lawrence, she hadn't gone out with many men and had always kept her distance emotionally. Lawrence had changed all that. But there were still times she felt so inept with the ways of men.

Checking her watch, Rachel noted the time was near for the reception. She knelt in front of Will and Sam and adjusted their clothes so their shirts were tucked into their pants and Sam's hair was combed into place. "I expect you two to be on your best behavior or we'll have to leave the reception. I'd like to stay to see who bids on my quilt. The money goes to a good charity to help children. After this we'll stop at your favorite fast-food restaurant for dinner before we head home. Okay?"

Both boys solemnly nodded their heads.

"Stay with me or Taylor. No wandering off."

They bobbed their heads again, overly enthusiastically.

As she stood, she rolled her eyes toward the ceiling and prayed for help to keep her twins in line. They had been so well-behaved all day that she was afraid they wouldn't be able to contain themselves much longer.

Max escorted her and the children toward the room where the reception was being held. Around the walls were long tables with sheets of paper before a photo of the quilts on display and up for the silent auction. Rachel took Will's hand while Taylor grabbed Sam's, then wandered around to see the bids. Rachel found hers. So far there was one amount down on the paper.

Will yanked on her arm. "I'm thirsty. And hungry."

"Let's go to the refreshment table and get something." As she walked away, she noticed Max stop in front of her bid sheet and write an amount down.

She quickly turned away before he caught her looking at him. After filling two cups with punch and getting a plate of goodies, she weaved her way through the crowd to Taylor who sat at a table with Sam. Will hopped up in the chair next to his sister and stuffed a small cookie into his mouth then washed it down with a gulp of the fruit drink, leaving a red ring around his mouth. Rachel gave him a napkin, and he wiped the juice off his face.

"Are we gonna be here long, Mom?" Taylor stared beyond Rachel.

She glanced over her shoulder to see Max approach. "We'll leave when the auction is finished. If you want to take your brothers to look at the decorated Christmas trees, you can. It should be about half an hour."

"Do you all want to see the trees?" Taylor finished off her punch.

"Yeah," Sam answered, followed by Will's affirmative.

"I'll bring them back in half an hour. You'll be here?"

As Rachel told her yes, Taylor snatched a last cookie from her plate and rose. After popping it into her mouth, she grasped the boys' hands and made her way toward the door.

"Alone at last," Max said and sat where Taylor had been.

"If you call being in a room with a hundred guests alone, then we are." Rachel finally took a chair next to Max.

"I'm impressed with your workmanship."

"Is that why you bid on my quilt?"

"I bid on it because I want it. The money goes to a good cause and I don't have anything for the holidays. It would look great on my couch. I never had a tree. I always worked on Christmas before so I didn't see any reason to buy ornaments and decorations."

"Then you'll have to keep an eye on the bid."

He snagged her gaze and held it for a long moment. "I intend to. I was hoping I could get you to help me do something for my lawn. I noticed all the neighbors have lights and decorations out. This morning I got a glare from my next-door neighbor. Not Doug but the other side. He wanted to know when I was putting up my lights."

"Oh, Harry really gets into it, but he's harmless. Just ignore him if you don't want to."

"If I'm gonna live in Tallgrass, I need to fit in." Max grasped her hand, rubbing his fingers into her palm. "Please. Your lawn is tastefully done."

"Fine," she said with a laugh at the hangdog expression he gave her.

"Great." He paused, his brow creasing. When he peered down at their hands clasped, he turned hers over and examined it. His pupils dilated. "You took off your wedding ring."

"Yes. I thought it was time." Her throat closed around those words. His tone—with a hint of incredulity—didn't exactly reassure her that she'd done the right thing. "Lawrence has been gone for two and a half years."

"I—I…"

The sound of the bell indicating ten minutes left to bid echoed through the large room.

"I'd better go over and stand near the bid sheet." He bolted to his feet and hurried away.

Rachel brought her hand to her face, feeling the warmth of his touch on her skin. She'd totally misread his interest. This just proved she didn't have a clue about men.

She took off her wedding ring. What does that mean? Max's hands on the steering wheel tightened until they ached.

He couldn't wait any longer to tell her why he was in Tallgrass. He'd wanted to know Taylor better—have a firmer foundation before he said anything, but he couldn't anymore. Once he told Rachel, their relationship would change—not for the good, but he didn't have any choice if he wanted to be in his daughter's life. And he wanted to be. Listening to her presentation on Louis Pasteur during her science class, he'd felt as if he'd actually helped her. That feeling had been something he wanted to experience again. And again.

Rachel deserved to know. He hated the thought they wouldn't even remain friends possibly. He cared about Rachel—perhaps too much, which was another reason he needed to tell her. He wasn't good at relationships, emotions. He'd messed up his marriage to Alicia to the point she'd kept the knowledge of his daughter from him.

"Mom, Will and Sam are taking up most of the backseat."

His daughter's voice cut into his thoughts, bringing him back to the present.

Rachel twisted around and peered at Taylor. "Hon, they're sleeping. We'll be home soon."

Taylor sighed loudly and stared out the side window. "Fine."

When Rachel turned back around, she caught his gaze lingering on her. He swiveled his attention toward the highway.

"I thought you were going to get into a fight with that woman at the reception," Rachel said, amusement woven through her words.

"I wasn't going to let her get the quilt." He chuckled. "She wasn't too happy when I bid a thousand dollars."

"Yeah, I noticed. She stomped off."

"It was worth every penny. It's for a good cause, and now I have a work of art I can display at Christmas." He started to ask her again about helping with decorating his lawn, but instead bit the inside of his mouth to keep the question inside. After this evening, they would be on opposite sides of a battle for Taylor.

The outskirts of Tallgrass came into view. The closer he neared their street the more his gut constricted into a huge knot. When he pulled into her driveway and parked her car in her garage, a taut band contracted about his chest, making each breath he drew in labored. He didn't want to hurt Rachel, but he didn't see any other way except silence. And he couldn't do that. In New York he'd toyed with that idea. Getting to know his daughter from afar. Being an observer only in his child's life.

But not now. This past month in her life only emphasized the impossibility of that.

Taylor hopped out of the car and headed for the door. Rachel scooped up Sam in her arms while Max carried Will into the house and up the stairs to his bedroom. He placed the boy on his bed, and he immediately curled onto his side and snuggled deeper into his pillow. Max removed the child's shoes and covered him with a blanket.

Straightening, he stared down at Will. What would it be like to have more than one child? He was still getting used to the idea of having a daughter, but he didn't think it would take much to want another. Once he'd dreamed of having a large family—with Alicia. The memory of her betrayal pierced his heart and opened the healing wound. If Alicia hadn't done what she'd done, he wouldn't be faced with telling Rachel about Taylor.

"Is Will still asleep?" Rachel asked behind him.

He pivoted toward her and nodded. The lump in his throat prevented him from saying anything. He swallowed several times.

"So is Sam. I used to drive them around to get them to sleep when they were babies. I guess it still works. Would you like some coffee or hot chocolate?"

"Hot chocolate sounds nice." He trudged toward the hallway, each step weighted down as though he dragged an iron ball on a chain behind him. The words he held inside burned in his gut and continued to jam his throat.

Rachel brought the two mugs full of hot chocolate to the kitchen table and set one down in front of Max. "Today was fun. I think all the kids enjoyed the trip, even Taylor. Did you see her eyes when she was at the elephant enclosure at the zoo?"

"I think she would have stayed there the whole time if it hadn't been for Will and Sam whining to go see the monkeys."

"Then all they did was race through so they could get to the snakes and birds."

"Yep, that about sums up the whole morning."

She sipped at her drink. "You were good with them. I don't sense any hostility from my daughter."

"Is she usually hostile to a new person?" Deep lines scrunched between his eyebrows.

"No, but I think at first she saw you replacing her father."

His lips pinched into a thin grimace. "Why?"

"Because you were taking over her father's office, working where he did. And…" She dropped her gaze from his.

"And what?"

"Since Lawrence died, I haven't been interested in a—" she curled her cold hands around her mug "—another man." Suddenly, the conversation was heading for shaky ground. Her mind swirled with different explanations of what she'd meant but she couldn't grasp any of them.

"Interested?"

The word, spoken in a husky rawness, lifted her gaze to his eyes, reconnecting with the dark green with flakes of gold in them. Her parched throat seized her voice, his look captured hers and bound her to him. She'd never been bold with a man, not even Lawrence, and how she'd all but practically told Max she was attracted to him. She wanted to take the declaration back.

"You are a special woman, Rachel." For a few seconds, softness grayed his eyes. "I shouldn't care as much…" Then the look faded to be replaced with a neutral expression as though he shielded his thoughts behind a blank facade. "I need to tell you something."

She held up her hand, palm outward. "First, I want to finish what I started. Yes, I'm interested in you. You're caring, kind. Taylor has responded to your help. We're following some of the strategies you've shared with us and they're working. And the boys look forward to you coming over. With that said, I'm not expecting anything from you. You don't have to feel obligated or anything. I'll still help you with decorating your lawn." She forced a lightness into her voice because the expression on his face worried her, as though she'd cornered him and demanded something he couldn't give. "I understand. Your wife recently died. It takes time to get over a close one's death, even if you were divorced. You two still shared a life together once."

He shoved back his chair, the scraping sound on the tile floor grating along Rachel's nerve endings. Shooting to his feet, he paced to the counter and put his mug into the sink. She squeezed her eyes closed, listening to his footsteps returning toward the table. When she peered up at him, hovering nearby, his jawline strengthened into a fierce countenance.

"My wife and I were divorced for thirteen years. Yes, she died recently, but I'm well over her and have been for a long time. But I'm not over what she did to me." Hurt flickered in and out of his eyes.

Rachel wanted to draw him to her, but his rigid stance forbade that. "What happened?"

"While I was serving in the army overseas, she divorced me. The only contact I had with her was through her lawyer. There was one thing she neglected to tell me when disclosing everything at the time of the divorce." He pulled in a deep breath, held it for a long moment then released it slowly. "She'd been pregnant with my child."

Her heart twisted like a bundle of barbed wire. "She raised your child without your knowledge?" Who had his child now?

"Not exactly. She put our daughter up for adoption without my knowledge." He backed away, leaning against the counter, his hands gripping its edge.

Suddenly staring into his bleak expression, she knew the answer. *Thirteen years ago. A girl. Could it be? No, that wasn't possible, Lord. Please tell me so.* "Where is she?"

"Here." His gaze clouded as though the sun glittering on the grass suddenly disappeared. "It's Taylor. She's my biological daughter. I never gave permission for her to be put up for adoption."

Her world fell away, the room spinning out of control. She squeezed her eyes shut to still its rotation. No, Max was lying. This was a trick. Lawrence had gone to college with the lawyer who handled the adoption. She tried to breathe, but fear seared her lungs, closing them off to any deep inhalations.

Clasping the table for support, she slowly lifted her eyelids and pierced him with a look she hoped conveyed her anger. "You don't know what you're talking about."

"The lawyer who handled the adoption was Charles Steward. Does that name sound familiar?"

She didn't have to see herself to know the color drained from her face. "But he's a good lawyer. A friend of my husband's."

"My wife didn't inform him who the father was. She said she didn't know and didn't want to raise a child."

"How do you know this?"

"From Alicia's sister."

"Why did she tell you finally about your daughter?" Suspicion laced each word, hope that he was mistaken weaving through her. Taylor was her daughter.

"She'd promised her sister she wouldn't say anything to me. She loved her older sister and believed everything Alicia told her about me and our marriage. But as Emily had children and saw how Alicia lived her life, she began to regret that promise. When Alicia died, she felt she wasn't bound to the vow she made to her sister anymore. She looked me up and came to see me to let me know."

"Did you talk with Charles Steward?"

"No. I got my information from Emily, some papers Alicia kept and a private investigator. I didn't want the man to alert you to my search."

Although she wasn't sure she could stand, she struggled to her feet, keeping her hands clasping the table to steady herself. "So, you decided to come and claim your daughter. And you expect me to hand her over without a fight?"

"No."

The concern in his eyes nearly melted her cold fury, but she couldn't allow that. She would do anything to keep her daughter. No one was going to come in and say she wasn't her child. No one. "You expect me to take your word for it?"

"No. I would like to do a DNA test so there is no doubt in your mind that I'm Taylor's father."

"No."

"Are you afraid I'm right?" He shoved away from the counter, his feet planted apart, his hands clenched at his sides.

A warrior's stance. As though he was readying himself to go to battle. She straightened, crossing her arms over her chest.

"I'll go to court to get it. Do you want your daughter to find out that way?"

"There is no good way to tell Taylor."

"Does she even know she's adopted?"

"Yes, she does. When she was old enough, I felt she had a right to know, but she didn't ever mention wanting to know anything about her biological parents."

A nerve in his jawline jerked. "We can quietly do the DNA test. I won't say anything to her until after the results come back." He took a step toward her, his expression gentling. "I don't want to hurt you, but I want to be in my daughter's life. She's my only child. One I didn't know about for thirteen years because my wife was vindictive. She wanted to get back at me because I had to fulfill my duty to my country and pay back the years they sent me to medical school. After she married me, she discovered she didn't want to be an army wife."

Another step and he was an arm's length away. Too close. She moved to the side. Needing a lot of space between them. She could hardly breathe as it was, but his nearness prodded her heartbeat to a quicker tempo. "I don't care. You can't disrupt Taylor's life like that."

"Do you think this is easy for me? I've agonized over how to do it. In the end, I decided there is no easy way."

"You could have stayed away."

He sucked in a ragged breath. "I considered that. When I had you investigated, I knew my daughter was with a good family, but that—"

"You had me investigated!" Her voice rose several levels at what he'd done.

"Shh, if you don't want Taylor to come in and find out like this."

Rachel snatched her coat from the hook on the wall by the utility room. "No, I don't want her to overhear us. Let's go outside and finish this conversation."

He grabbed his jacked and shrugged into it. "Fine. Where do you suggest?"

"The front porch."

Max trod toward the foyer and wrenched open the front door. She followed him outside and went to the far end of the porch, mostly hidden from the street by large bushes. She certainly didn't want the whole neighborhood to see them either, but going to his house wasn't an option. Battling on his home turf wasn't a wise strategy.

He leaned back against a post, the twinkling clear lights decorating the front of her house throwing his face into shadows. "I had you investigated so I would know what I was getting into. I wanted to know all I could about Taylor's situation. I knew she was struggling in school before I came."

"So, you think I'm not doing a good job with her?" The very idea sent terror through her. She might not be perfect, but she was doing everything she could. No one could doubt her love for Taylor.

"I didn't say that, and no, I don't think that. I know raising children, especially teenagers, isn't easy."

She wanted to shout at him, "How do you know? You haven't raised a child." But she kept those words inside that begged to be released in her anger.

"I've seen a lot with patients I've dealt with. I've been part of a counseling program for teens in New York. It has given me a perspective others may not have."

"So, you think you can do a better job?"

"I didn't say that, either." He clamped his jaws, the hard set of his face underscoring his own rising anger. Tearing his gaze from her, he raked his fingers through his hair. "Let's take this one step at a time. Get the test done, then you and I will discuss what to do next. We could look at sharing custody. We—"

Custody! The word struck fear through her heart. Losing Taylor would rip her family apart. Would rip her apart. "I'm not agreeing to anything until I talk with my lawyer first."

"Fine. I'll give you until Friday before I pursue this in court." He headed toward her and paused next to her. "I will be in my daughter's life. You can't change that."

When he left her alone on the porch, she collapsed into the swing, her legs no longer able to hold her up. She scrubbed her trembling hands down her face, kneading her fingertips into her temple that throbbed. This was a nightmare.

Lord, what do I do? How do I handle this? How could You let this happen to me? I could lose Taylor.

Chapter Nine

"I'm so glad Taylor could work with Becca's children and Nicholas this morning here. I don't know if I could have corralled her enough to get her to do any work today." Rachel sat in Jordan's kitchen, nursing her fifth cup of coffee after a night of not sleeping. Every time she closed her eyes, she saw her daughter being wrenched from her arms by Max.

"What did the lawyer say?"

"That this could get ugly, and I should first establish if Max is the biological father."

"So you're gonna agree to the DNA test?"

"I don't see a choice here. I need to know, especially if he tries to take me to court over this. I even considered leaving Tallgrass and living somewhere else."

Pupils dilated, Jordan gasped. "You've considered that?"

"Frankly, yes, until I talked with my lawyer this morning. I can't do it to my family. Besides, Taylor would want to know why we were leaving. Why we were never coming back to Tallgrass. I know from my lawyer that the court would probably rule in my favor, but Taylor has been having problems. What if they decide in Max's favor?" Rachel took a swallow of the caffeine-laced drink. Her eyes burned from the lack of sleep.

"What are you going to say to Taylor?"

"She knows she was adopted. Five years ago, Lawrence and I had a long conversation about why we adopted her. She hasn't asked any questions since then. I don't want to say anything unless she is Max's child."

Jordan went to the stove and retrieved the pot. Back at the table, she refilled her mug as well as Rachel's. "So, you're going to wait until the DNA test comes back. I think that's best. What if Max isn't Taylor's father? Why upset her and throw her life in turmoil if he isn't?"

"My point exactly." The warmth from Rachel's cup seeped into her icy fingers. "I called and asked him to come to my house this afternoon during his lunch break to settle this."

"What are you gonna do if he's Taylor's father?"

The very idea seared a hole through her stomach. Her heart ached, a tautness about her chest. "I don't know. All I know is that I can't lose my daughter."

Jordan's mouth hardened into a frown. "You aren't gonna lose her. I've been praying. We'll get others— Mom, Granny—"

"No, I don't want anyone else but you and the lawyer knowing about this until the test comes back. The less people who know, the less likelihood someone would let it slip. Taylor is struggling enough right now."

"How can Max do this?"

Rachel had asked herself that question many times since she'd discovered his intentions last night. "I'm trying to put myself in his shoes and see it from his point of view. But I can't right now. I'm so angry at him."

Jordan clasped her hand. "You cared about him. You weren't expecting that from him."

"I took my wedding ring off because I thought there might be something developing between us. What a fool I was!"

"You're not. You have a big heart. Stop by before you pick up Taylor today and let me know how the meeting went."

Rachel inhaled a deep, calming breath, but her chest still hurt. "Will do. I'd better get going."

When Rachel rose, Jordan gave her a hug. "I'm here for you."

"I know. I'm blessed to have my family."

And that was the problem. She understood how important family was. When she thought about Max, she saw loneliness in his eyes. That was the first thing that had drawn her to him.

But he can't have Taylor to appease that loneliness.

"So, you told her about Taylor?"

Brendan's voice floated to Max, reminding him of the evening before. Max gripped his cell tighter. "Yeah, and I wish I hadn't."

"Why? The DNA test needs to be done so you can proceed forward with what you want."

What I want? The problem was it was two conflicting things. "I didn't want to hurt Rachel." *Because I care about her more than I should. She's nothing like my ex-wife.*

"But you knew you were going to have to. You shouldn't have gotten to know her so well. That has made this whole situation harder."

His brother was only telling him what he'd already concluded during the middle of a sleepless night. "I can't undo what's been done. I'm meeting her in a few minutes to discuss Taylor."

"Don't forget after what Alicia did to you that you deserve a chance with your daughter."

At a cost to Rachel? Her family? Maybe even his child? He knew in his heart he was Taylor's father, especially after piecing everything together from Alicia's papers, what her sister had told him and the timing of his deployment right before Alicia asked for a divorce. "First the DNA testing."

"Maybe you could bring Taylor back to New York to visit at Christmas. We'd love to meet her."

"No! I won't do that to her even if we get the results back fast."

"Yeah, I guess the courts don't move that fast, especially around the holidays."

"And they might not rule in my favor." In fact, probably wouldn't, but that wouldn't stop him from trying if he had to. "This may not be settled for quite some time."

"Keep me posted."

"I will. Give my love to your family. Talk to you later." Max disconnected the call and slipped his cell back into his pocket.

Family. Would he ever have one? Was this the way to go? When he'd seen Rachel's expression last night—so full of hurt and fear, all directed at him, he'd doubted his plan to be in his daughter's life. He didn't want to do more harm. But he wanted to see his child grow up. He'd already missed thirteen years. Thirteen precious years he could never reclaim.

"Come in." Rachel opened the door all the way and stepped to the side.

"Is Taylor here?" Max entered her house, the dark circles under his eyes attesting to his sleepless night.

Good. She would hate to think he'd slept while she hadn't. How could she when she was faced with such a dilemma? "She's at the ranch. I didn't want her here when we talk." She gestured toward the formal living room with its white furniture.

"Did you talk to a lawyer today?"

"Yes, and he suggested I go through with the DNA testing although there's a good chance the court would rule that Taylor should stay with me." It was important she made the point she didn't think she would lose Taylor even if he were her father. "And I agree with my lawyer. We need to find out first if she is your daughter." Her legs shaking, she sat on the couch.

"I don't want to take this to court." He remained standing, the coffee table between them.

His chances legally weren't good, so she could understand why he'd said that. Why was he pursuing his claim? What was he up to? "That wasn't the impression you gave me last night. So what do you want?" Her hands clasped together, she placed them in her lap and forced a calm tone. "Please have a seat."

He folded his long length into the chair across from the couch. "As I said yesterday, I want to be involved in Taylor's life."

"My lawyer told me it would be better if we could work something out, but if I have to go to court, I'm prepared to."

"And put your daughter through a nasty fight?"

"I'm not the one who is pushing this. You are." Rachel crossed her arms over her chest.

"So, if the test comes back that I'm her natural father, what do you have in mind?"

"That we continue as before. You are a friend of the family. Taylor was warming to you."

"Oh, I see. We live a charade."

When he put it that way, it bothered Rachel. She never lied to her daughter and didn't relish spending the next years doing that very thing. And what if when she was older, she decided to look for her biological parents? "What do you suggest?"

"Full disclosure. I think Taylor needs to know I'm her father and that I didn't have any knowledge of her until recently." Rachel started to speak when Max held up his hand. "Through no fault of you and your husband. I want her to know about her biological family, too, and I hope she'll allow me to be in her life. I won't force her. I didn't come here to disrupt everything."

"What did you think was going to happen?"

He looked her in the eye for a long moment. "I didn't really think it through as much as I should have. At first, I just wanted to see her and make sure everything was all right. I wanted to get to know her. Things changed as we got to know each other. I realized I wanted more."

"You can't replace Lawrence in her life."

"I don't want to. He was an important part of her life, and I wouldn't want to take away from that."

"So, what do we do about the DNA testing? I don't want Taylor to know about it until we get the results."

"The lab can get DNA from a hair sample. Can you take some from her brush?"

"Okay." Rachel stood. "What do I do?"

"Let's get the brush and come over to my house. I have the paperwork almost completely filled out. We can finish it up and send it to the lab. Together, so there are no doubts on our parts."

"You really have trust issues, don't you?"

He slipped his gaze away and stared into the foyer.

"Can you blame me after what Alicia did? I was burned. It only takes me once to want to avoid the fire."

"Believe it or not, I'm sorry your ex-wife did what she did. Nothing good ever comes out of such hatred. But—" she sucked in a deep breath and released it slowly "—I will protect my daughter at all costs. I want your promise you'll put Taylor first in whatever we discover."

"I won't knowingly set out to hurt Taylor."

"But you won't promise?"

"Putting Taylor first may mean two different things to us. I don't want you to think I'll back off from getting to know my daughter just because you say so."

In her dealings with Max he'd always seemed fair and rational. Could she put her trust in him to do the right thing by Taylor? *Lord, what do I do?*

No answer other than what they had decided came to mind. Maybe that was her answer. Trust the Lord to know what was best.

Max answered his phone in his den, noting the number was Rachel's. "Max, Will's sick, and I can't get hold of Mom at the church."

Taylor's frantic voice bolted Max to his feet. "What's wrong?" He started for his front door with his mobile phone plastered to his ear.

"Nana and Granny aren't home, and I'm babysitting Will and Sam."

"I'll be over to see about Will. I'm heading out the door now." Max grabbed his medical bag he kept for emergencies and headed across the street to Rachel's.

Taylor stood in the entrance waiting for him. Worry slashed her eyebrows downward. "Mom's at her quilting group at church. They usually meet in a classroom. I don't know why she isn't answering her cell. It went to voice mail. It's not like Mom not to have her cell on. But the past couple of days she's been upset."

And he was the reason she was upset. Guilt nibbled at him. "Where's Will?"

"Upstairs in his bed. He's hot. I took his temperature and it's 103 degrees. That's bad, isn't it?"

Max mounted the steps, turning back to ask Taylor, "How's Sam?"

"He's watching TV in the den. I'll go check on him. You know which room is Will's?"

"Yeah," Max said from the top of the staircase.

Ten minutes later, Max had checked Will and determined it was the flu going around. He didn't want to give the boy anything for his fever until he could get hold of Rachel. When Taylor came into Will's bedroom, she wore a frown and held Sam's hand.

"I think he's getting the same thing as Will. He says he doesn't feel well."

Max took Sam's temperature, asked him some question about what was wrong, then had Taylor take her brother to his room.

Max retrieved his cell and tried Rachel's number. Maybe this time she would answer. When it went to voice mail, he left a message, then called Eileen to see if she was home yet. No answer. He walked to Will's window that overlooked the street and noticed that the porch light was now on at Doug's house. Hopefully, they had returned home.

He hurried to Sam's bedroom and asked, "What's Granny's number?" He punched it in as Taylor recited it.

Doug answered on the second ring and got his wife.

"Can you come over and watch Sam and Will? I need to go to church and get Rachel." Max explained why and Granny said she and Doug would be over right away.

Max made his way downstairs with Taylor following.

"I'm coming with you."

"You'd better stay here and help Granny and Doug. I shouldn't be long. The church is only ten minutes away."

"Will they be all right?"

He placed his hands on her shoulders. "Your brothers will be fine. It's the flu that's going around. They have the same symptoms as the patients I've been seeing. It'll run its course. Have them drink some water if you can to keep them hydrated," he said to give her something to do.

Granny thrust the door open and invaded the house, using her cane to walk faster. Doug was right behind her. "Are Will and Sam upstairs?"

"Yes, Granny. I can keep an eye on them until Mom gets home. I know the stairs can be—"

Granny blew past Taylor, making a beeline for the steps. "Nonsense, child. I'm perfectly capable of managing the stairs when I need to."

"Here, let me help you." Max moved to assist her.

Granny paused, gave him a cutting look then proceeded without him. "You're wasting time, young man. Get Rachel."

Max winked at Taylor. "Be back soon." He glanced back to make sure Rachel's grandmother was progressing up the staircase all right. She was halfway up with Doug at her elbow. The sight of those two devoted to each other, in love, heightened his loneliness.

Rachel sat in the front pew in the sanctuary, taking a break from working on the quilt after poking herself with a needle several times because she couldn't keep her mind on her work. It would be weeks before she and Max got the results on the DNA testing. Weeks of anguish worrying. Weeks of wondering what was the right thing to do.

She needed the peace she always found in here. She'd taken her wedding ring off because she'd been attracted to Max—cared about him as more than just friends. She'd done the right thing today by sending off Taylor's DNA with Max's. Even though she had a good chance of winning any case that went to court concerning her daughter, how could she live with herself without knowing the truth one way or another? Then she could deal with it.

Is this a test, Father? I'm not going to turn away from You. But I do need to know You are with me, that I'm doing what is right in Your eyes. I can't even begin to see why You did this, but You must have a good reason. Help me to see it.

As she sat there, that sense of calm she sought blanketed her. She would take it one step at a time. She closed her eyes and pictured a meadow with a gentle breeze blowing the wildflowers in full bloom in ripples like a wave on an ocean. She could smell their clean, fresh scent swirling around her. She could feel the warming rays of the sun bathing her face. Peace.

Finally, she stood and made her way toward the church classroom where the women in the quilting club were working. Now she could concentrate on what she needed to do.

"Rachel, your purse has been vibrating," her mother's best friend, Anna, said when Rachel entered the room.

"Must be my cell." She crossed to her purse sitting on the floor along the wall. When she withdrew it, she noticed she had two messages. She listened to Taylor's frantic one. "Will's got a high fever." Her heart rate kicked up several notches as she grabbed her bag. "I've got to go. Will is sick."

"Rachel, wait…"

So upset, Rachel didn't wait to hear what Anna had to say. As she hurried down the hallway, she played the second message. Max's deep voice, level, matter-of-fact, immediately quieted her worst fears. "Taylor called me and I came over to check on Will, who has the flu going around. His fever is 103 degrees, and he's complaining of aches and being tired. Call me. I'd like to give him something for the fever."

Rachel hit the parking lot at a fast clip, trying to punch in Max's number at the same time. Suddenly, bright car lights flooded the area. She looked toward the vehicle pulling up. Max's Mustang. Relief eased her tensed muscles.

He came to a stop next to her and rolled down his window. "Will and Sam are going to be fine. Hop in. I'll give you a ride."

"I can drive myself. I…" Suddenly, she realized she'd gotten a ride with her mom's friend. Her car was still in her garage. "I forgot Anna brought me." She quickly rounded the front of the Mustang and climbed into the passenger seat. She threw a sheepish smile at Max. "I'm sure that was what Anna was going to tell me as I hurried from the room."

Anna came barreling out of the church door, clasping her purse to her chest. When she saw Rachel in Max's car, Anna waved and turned back into the building.

"Tell me one of my children is sick and that's all I can think of." She twisted toward him. "Hey, wait. You said Will *and* Sam are going to be all right."

"Sam isn't feeling well either. His fever isn't as high.

But I didn't give either one anything for their fever without your permission. You should when you get home."

"I should have known something was wrong before I left. Will was quietly playing on his bed. Not like him."

"Granny and Doug are over at the house with Taylor."

"Why did Taylor bother you?"

"When she couldn't get hold of you, she tried her grandmother and Granny. Neither answered so she called me. Your mom is still gone."

"She's probably out Christmas shopping. She likes to have it done before Thanksgiving but didn't this year."

When Max pulled into Rachel's driveway, she pushed the door open, saying, "Thanks for the ride and helping out."

Without waiting for a reply, she strode toward her house, anxious to see for herself that her twins were okay. She heard a car door slam shut, but she didn't look back to see if Max was coming inside. There was a part of her that would be glad if he followed her, but the other part didn't know what to make of him. And she didn't have time to figure it out right now.

Later that evening, after Rachel had settled her two sons in bed, their fever down, she went in search of Max, who'd stayed in case she needed any help. When she'd said she had everything under control, Taylor had piped in that she needed help with her math problems she still had to do. Max quickly volunteered, and they sat at the game table in the den to work.

Rachel paused in the doorway and observed the pair. Her daughter bent over her notepad, her tongue sticking out of the corner of her mouth, something she did when she concentrated on what she was doing.

"Are you sure that number goes there?" Max had loosened his tie he'd been wearing earlier and had rolled up his long-sleeve blue shirt to the elbows.

He gave off a casual, at-home look that made Rachel catch her breath. He peered up at her and snagged her full attention. Why hadn't she seen it before? Taylor's eyes look exactly like his—the same color, the same slant. Her throat closed. She remained perched in the entrance as though any second she would spin around and flee.

Taylor glanced up from studying her paper. "No and since you asked, I guess it doesn't go there."

"Actually, it does. I just wanted to make sure you felt it should. You seemed to hesitate."

Taylor flashed a grin. "That's the second time you've tried to trick me."

"I want you to think about your moves, understand the reason why you do it. Once you do, math will come much easier to you."

Taylor saw Rachel. "How's Will and Sam?"

"They're doing what they need to get better—sleeping." Rachel finally took several steps into the den, aware Max's attention was fixed on her.

"That sounds good to me right now." Yawning, Taylor gathered up her notepad and algebra book. "Thanks for helping me, Max. I was sure glad you were home earlier. I figured out one thing tonight. I don't want to be a doctor like Dad. I didn't like seeing Will and Sam sick." Hopping up, she snatched up her belongings and walked toward the doorway.

Rachel noticed the color fade from his tanned features

when Taylor mentioned her father. "I won't be far behind you, Taylor. Today has been a long and tiring day."

As Taylor left, Max scooted back his chair and rose. "Not one I want to repeat anytime soon." He snapped his fingers. "I almost forgot. Your mom called when she heard the message from Taylor on her machine. She said she would be up for a while if you need her. I told her the twins would be fine with rest."

"I wonder where she was. She's usually home most nights, especially Wednesdays and Thursdays."

"I know where she was." The twinkle in his eyes sparkled like dew on grass.

"Are you going to make me guess?"

"Normally, I would, but since it's been a long, tiring day, I'll tell you. She had a date with Kevin. I think he was still there. I thought I heard a male voice in the background."

"She did? She didn't say anything to me."

"Kevin didn't say anything to me, either."

"Maybe it wasn't a date." Rachel ambled into the hallway and toward the front door.

"Would that bother you if it was?"

She stopped in the foyer and shifted toward him. "No. It's about time my mother dated and enjoyed the company of a man. She's only gone on a few dates over the years since my father left her."

"She's an attractive woman. I'm surprised she hasn't gone out much."

"My mother's choice. Let's just say when my father walked out she didn't want a repeat of that experience and decided to focus on her career and raising Jordan and me."

"I guess I, of all people, can understand her reasons."

"Because of what happened to your marriage?"

He nodded, a solemn expression puckering his brow. "Like your mom, I don't want to repeat that experience. No matter what my heart feels."

A softening in his gaze rooted her to the floor. Did he mean he had feelings for her? "Not all marriages end badly. I had a good one."

"And you want to repeat the experience?"

The question hung in the air between them, charging it with emotions that rushed to the surface. Did she? She hadn't thought she would ever get a second chance since she'd been blessed to have one good marriage. As much as she wanted to tell him no after all that had transpired between them, she couldn't say the word. Her ringless left hand underscored her desire to move on. "It was a good time in my life. I miss that closeness. Wouldn't anyone?"

His smile was slow to come, but it reached deep into his eyes. "But some people are optimistic and are sure things will be better the second attempt."

"But not you?"

"I'm more of a realist. I've seen too much to think otherwise."

"When you worked in the emergency room?"

"That and in war zones."

She tilted her head. "Why are you here?"

Max panned the area behind her. His eyebrows sliced downward. "You know why," he said in a low voice.

"I think it's more than that." She covered the distance to the front door, opened it and stepped out onto the porch. "What are you searching for?"

His frown strengthened. "What do you want me to say?"

"The answer to the question." Tension poured off him. She treaded in territory he wanted left untouched. But if he was Taylor's father—she couldn't deny the similarities she'd seen—she wanted to know the real Max Connors, not the person he showed the world.

"I want…" He snapped his mouth closed and stared at a spot to her left. His Adam's apple bobbed several times. "I want to get to know my daughter."

"Besides that. There's something else driving you. What?"

Chapter Ten

"I want peace."

The ragged thread of Max's voice held Rachel immobile.

"I've seen so much death. I want to see life. I worked at a hospital that saw a lot of the seedy side—murder, gang fights, humans preying on humans. I thought I could handle it after what I'd done in the army serving at the front lines. It didn't prepare me, or rather I couldn't any longer ignore what it was doing to me."

In that moment, everything that had happened in the past couple of days between them vanished. She couldn't stand there and hear the depth of his anguish and not care.

"When I found out about Taylor, I thought it was my chance to make a change. I actually thought the Lord had sent me a second chance. I'd messed up my marriage. I'd stopped talking to Alicia. I was as much at fault for the marriage failing as she was. When she asked for a divorce, I was relieved because I didn't know what else to do to make things the way they were when we first dated and married."

"People don't stay the same. The fact you got married

changes who you are. You become a team, finding ways to work together."

His arms stiff at his sides, he curled and uncurled his hands. "Alicia and I never did. That was the problem. Then I was gone more and more because I was deployed several times. At first she was upset, and even when she could come with me overseas, she refused to. Then later she just didn't care if I was there or not. I won't go through that again."

His declaration erected a barrier between them as though he had posted a "Do Not Disturb" sign around his heart. And yet, Rachel decided she wouldn't give up. If Taylor were his daughter, no matter what she wanted, they would be connected. Before she wanted to get to know him, possibly beyond friendship, because she'd been attracted to him. Still was. Now, though, she needed to know the type of man who'd sired her child. Might be in her life? How could she deny her daughter a dad if Taylor wanted a relationship with Max?

She'd gotten the impression he was angry with God. Maybe she could change that, give him that second chance he was talking about—at least with the Lord. "You mentioned you thought coming here was a second chance, that the Lord may have had a hand in it. Come with us to church on Sunday. It'll be Taylor's first performance with the choir."

His eyes brightened, the stress melting from his stance. "I'd like that."

"Then in the afternoon we can help you decorate your yard. I wouldn't want the neighbors to band against you. In case you haven't noticed, your house is the only one not decorated on the street. Even Doug has some lights out."

"I noticed, but I've got the decoration problem taken

care of. I'm getting it tomorrow and putting it out Saturday." He turned to leave, stopped in midmotion and peered back at her. "Call if the boys get worse. I can be here quickly."

"I appreciate you being here for my children."

One corner of his mouth tilted upward. "Anytime."

As he left, she realized he'd meant that about being here for her and the kids. In five weeks he'd become a frequent visitor to her house. Of course, now she knew why. It hadn't been because he'd been interested in her. Only Taylor. At least in the past twenty-four hours she'd learned not to lose her heart to Max. And tonight he'd reinforced the reasons why he couldn't commit to a woman.

On his porch, the security light illuminating him, he swung around and looked directly at her. Suddenly, it seemed as though only a few feet separated them rather than yards. She needed to harden her heart to his appeal. There was no future for them except where her daughter was concerned. Breaking the visual bond, she moved toward her front door.

In the back pew next to Rachel, Max listened to the choir sing. Taylor's face, full of joy, kept his attention riveted. He loved to sing, too. He'd even fancied himself being in a band when he was a teenager. Had she gotten her musical ability from him? The thought made him smile.

He knew the DNA test would come back a match. And when it did, he had decisions to make. Should he try to take Rachel to court over Taylor or work something out with Rachel? He knew realistically and legally she had a strong case of retaining full custody of Taylor. But knowing that hadn't stopped him from searching for his daughter and trying to become part of her life.

The music swelled to its end. Max looked sideways at the woman sitting next to him. She had so much to offer a man. She made him want to see if a relationship beyond friendship could work for him. He certainly wasn't blind to her attractive qualities, and yet becoming involved with her might complicate an already complicated situation.

He needed to keep focused on developing a relationship with his daughter not her mother—no matter how beautiful she was on the inside and outside.

At the end, Rachel rose, taking Will's hand while Sam fit his in Max's grasp. "What did you think?"

"I think Taylor loves to sing."

"Well, yes, but about the service?"

"Your pastor is good. He's given me something to think about." Remembering the sermon on putting trust in the Lord even during the tough times caused Max to pause. Had he given up on God when he should have leaned on Him? Was Pastor John right that the Lord didn't give people more than they could handle?

"I'm glad. You can come anytime you want with us." Rachel filed out of the pew and waited for him.

The invitation gave him hope that somehow they could work out the situation with Taylor. He wouldn't stop until he had explored every option available to him. Being around Rachel's family emphasized how much he had missed over the years. "I may take you up on that."

He stood in line with Rachel to greet Pastor John. Jordan, Zachary and Nicholas were behind them. Soon Granny, Doug, Eileen and Kevin joined them, quickly followed by Taylor. Surrounded by the members of

Rachel's family further heightened the hope he suddenly felt. Was it the place or the people or both?

"Pastor John, I'd like you to meet a—" a slight pause from Rachel before she finished with "—a friend. Dr. Max Connors. He's Kevin's new partner."

The pastor pumped Max's arm with a firm handshake. "It's good to see you here. We sorely needed another doctor."

"I know. I thought I would ease into the job, but instead I've plunged headfirst. I've been busier here than a Saturday night in the emergency room in New York City."

"I can imagine. No matter what precautions we make, the flu seems to make its rounds. I hope to see you here often." Pastor John bent down and passed a lollipop to each of the twins, then greeted Taylor with a big smile. "I enjoyed seeing you in the choir. Such talent is always welcomed."

As Max moved toward the foyer, Taylor beamed, her shoulders thrust back, her stance tall. Her self-esteem had taken a hit with her struggles in school, especially with reading. But in the past month with Rachel working with her on phonetics and flash cards of common words, Taylor's fluency had increased, her confidence had grown. The occasional times he'd worked with her on science she didn't get as frustrated as she had at first.

Rachel came up to his side, her hand brushing his arm before it fell away as though she suddenly realized she was touching him. "Do you mind if we go to the rec hall for refreshments before we leave?"

"I'm just along for the ride. Whatever you want to do."

"If I could only get my kids to say that, I'd have it

made." She started for the double doors that led to the reception after the service. "I noticed you had a big blow-up snowman out in front of your house. Do you plan on doing anything else?"

"Mr. Olson didn't say anything last night about my house being the only one without decorations, so I'm thinking that's all I need."

"You do? Then you don't know Mr. Olson well enough."

"What do you mean?"

"Do you know those Christmas movies that show neighbors having wars over decorating their yards? Well, no doubt they use Mr. Olson as the model for the character who started them in the first place."

When they reached the rec hall, Max released Sam's hand and the child raced toward the refreshment table. "That doesn't surprise me. I think I should have been warned when I bought my house."

"The Realtor saw you were from out of town. She isn't dumb," Rachel said with a chuckle and let go of Will, who quickly followed his brother. "Mr. Olson has quite a reputation in Tallgrass. Every year he adds to his yard. I'm just glad he lives at the other end of the block. I know the people around him have gotten black-out curtains because the lights are so bright. He wants our street to be the place people come during December to see the Christmas decorations. The only reason I have any to put out at all is because Lawrence got wrapped up in trying to outdo Mr. Olson. He never could."

As Max moved through the line, he picked up some cookies, chips and dip and half a turkey sandwich. "In New York, I never had to worry about decorations. I didn't even put up a tree. I wasn't there enough to justify the time and expense."

"And now?"

"I want to start some holiday traditions."

"Any thoughts which ones?"

"No, but I have a feeling you're an expert. Didn't you tell me once you really get into the Christmas season?"

"Yes, but probably not quite like you think."

"What?"

"Oh, no, I don't want to tell you. I'd rather show you. My lips are sealed." She did a twisting motion in front of her mouth as though she were locking it.

But what lured Max was the sight of her full, red lips. Beckoning him to kiss them. Her gaze connected with his and bound him to her. The image of her in his embrace, their mouths joined together, no space between them, filled his mind.

"Hey, you two, you're holding up the line. Some of us are hungry."

Jordan tapped him on the shoulder and pulled him back to the present in the middle of the church's rec hall with a room full of people milling about. Heat flushed Max's cheeks. He inched forward, trying to rid his mind of the picture that kept haunting him.

To cover his embarrassment, Max latched on to the first thing he saw as he looked away from Rachel. "Is that the quilt you told me that you made depicting Christ's life?"

"Yes. The group at church I belong to finished it right before Thanksgiving. Our gift to the congregation. Now we're working on something else."

Max again fixed his full attention on Rachel. "Beautiful." And that word wasn't just referring to the quilt although it was expertly done.

* * *

"Where's my snowman? It's not in my yard." Max hopped out of Rachel's car the second she stopped in her driveway. He strode toward the sidewalk, noticing his stakes still planted in the ground in front.

Wind whipping her hair, Rachel approached him, pointing down the street. "Isn't that it? It's in Mom's yard."

At that moment, her mother pulled up to her house and got out of her car, her hands planted on her waist. She stared at the big white round bottom of the snowman on its side. It had flattened part of her manger scene. Mary and Joseph lay on their side, baby Jesus somewhere in the white folds of Max's decoration that was losing its air. Part of the top hat flapped in the wind, but the majority of the body was snagged on the edge of the manger.

Her mom turned and cupped her hands to her mouth, shouting, "Do something before it ruins everything."

Max jogged toward her while Rachel trailed at a more sedate pace in her high heels. The snowman finally broke loose from the manger and tumbled toward the stand of lighted circular pine trees with fake deer grazing among them in Mr. Olson's side yard. Max dove the last couple of feet and grabbed for a handful of that snowman to keep it from invading the property of the man who had started it all.

Max landed in the middle of a sea of white. Clutching the material, he struggled to his feet. The snowman's arms flailed in the brisk breeze and knocked into him, sending him back down in an attempt to swallow him in a cocoon of snow. This time he snatched fistfuls of the decoration until it was deflated like a limp balloon.

Rachel stood with her mother near the chaos at the

manger and watched Max fight for control of his snowman. "Do you think I should help?"

"Nah. Let him. Maybe then he'd appreciate a more subtle touch in decorating and let you help him with it. Even I thought it was a bit much."

"You mean huge. It sort of reminded me of the Pillsbury Doughboy about to annihilate New York City."

Her mother tossed back her head and laughed.

Max glared at them. "I could use some help."

"Are you sure?" Rachel pressed her lips together to keep from joining her mom in merriment.

He dragged some more white material into his arms, fighting the decoration as much as the wind. "Yes."

Rachel skirted the ballooning decoration and started with the top hat. Moving toward Max on the ground, she gathered as much as she could until she reached Max, who sat on a good portion of his errant display to harness it.

"Do you have a Plan B?"

"For the yard?" He peered toward his now barren lawn with four stakes still sticking up out of the brown grass. "Maybe I could go back and get a smaller snowman or something."

"How about 'or something'?"

"What do you suggest?"

"I have leftover some green and red lights from my husband's stash of outdoor decorations. Just something simple will be enough. Bigger isn't better."

Max pushed off the ground and stood. "I want to know how this got away." After folding as much of the material as possible, he tramped toward his house with some of it trailing behind him.

Taylor, Will and Sam ran across the street to join Max. Rachel paused next to her mother.

"He doesn't understand about Christmas, does he?"

Rachel shook her head. "But he's asked me to help him."

"That's a good start. It was nice seeing him in church today. I've got the feeling he's here in Tallgrass for a reason beyond working with Kevin."

"You do?" Rachel studied her mother's face, a thoughtful expression in her eyes.

"I think we can help him. Or at least you can. He's hurting. I see it sometimes when he doesn't think anyone is looking."

If her mother only knew. She didn't want to say anything to anyone until after the DNA test results came back. No sense alarming her family if there was no reason to. "I'll try to do my best."

"I noticed you took off your wedding ring. Does this mean you're interested in him?"

"No." Yes, but his revelation changed everything. "Don't you think it's time I said goodbye to Lawrence?"

"It's only time when you're ready. I do think Will and Sam could use a father figure."

"You didn't think that when Jordan and I were growing up. What's changed your view?"

At that moment, Kevin's Cadillac pulled into her mother's driveway.

She smiled. "He has."

"Oh, no. First Granny, then Jordan and now you. Am I going to have to suffer through you all trying to fix me up with a man?"

"Nope, dear. I would never do that to you." Her mom sauntered toward Kevin, who climbed from his sedan and greeted her with a light kiss on the mouth.

Rachel strolled toward Max's house, where her

children circled him, all staring down at a stake. Max held one of the tethers in his hand.

"Did you find out what happened?" she asked as she crossed his yard.

He pivoted, his face crumpled into an angry expression. "The lines were cut. At least three of them. One snapped, I guess in the wind. I've been sabotaged!"

"Mom, who would do something like that?" With one hand on her hip, her daughter scanned the houses on the street, upset as if it had happened to her.

At that moment, Rachel saw Mr. Olson park his black truck in his driveway and get out of it. He glanced toward them, smiling, and waved, then headed toward his porch. She thought she saw a skip to his walk.

Max came up to her and whispered, "He wouldn't, would he?"

She shrugged. "No way to tell, but I wouldn't let it bother you. I've got a solution. My offer of lights still stands."

"You don't think I should go out and buy something?"

"I've got more than enough for you. Remember, we're neighbors and neighbors help each other in Tallgrass."

"I'm not sure Mr. Olson got the memo."

"If he's responsible for this, he has to live with that."

"Forgive and forget?"

"Much easier on your stress level." Rachel shifted toward Taylor. "Hon, you know where we keep our extra outdoor lights in the garage. Will you get the red and green ones for me? We're going to help Max fix his yard up."

"Can we help?" Sam asked, hopping up and down as though they hadn't been sick a few days ago.

"I thought you were going to help Granny bake Christmas cookies this afternoon."

"Oh, yeah. She needs a taster." Will grabbed hold of Sam's arm and tugged him toward Granny's house. "We'll see when she wants us."

"Now that we're alone, what should I really do about Mr. Olson?" Max asked, glaring at the man's place as though his look could burn it down.

"Exactly what I said. Let it go. I actually feel sorry for Mr. Olson, who thinks Christmas is about how big his decorations are. He doesn't understand Christmas is a time to welcome Jesus into our lives. To reaffirm what Christ wants us to do, love our neighbors as ourselves."

"Does this mean you forgive me for keeping the reason I came to Tallgrass a secret for a month?"

"Being angry at you won't change the facts. If it could, I would. Instead, we'll have to figure out what to do when we know for sure. I don't want a court battle if possible. But I won't lose Taylor, either. I'll do what I need to."

"So will I." A grim twist to his mouth whipped through her like the chill to the wind blowing.

The progress they'd made the past few days suddenly slipped away. She glimpsed Taylor coming back across the street carrying a box with the word *lights* in big, black letters on its side.

"Please for our sakes and Taylor's, let's agree to forget about it until after the holidays and we get the results back."

He swung his attention toward Taylor, grinning. "A deal. Believe or not, I don't want to fight, either."

Rachel blew out a breath slowly as if she were defusing herself.

"Mom, there's another box in the garage."

"I'll get it." Max loped toward her house.

"Where are we gonna start?" Taylor placed the carton on the ground.

"Let's alternate red and green lights and string them along the sidewalk that leads to his porch. Then we can put some along the porch. After that, we'll see what we have left."

"I'm gonna miss the Jolly White Snowman."

"Not me. It was an eyesore."

Taylor stared at her. "You didn't cut the lines, did ya?"

"If only I had thought of it." Rachel chuckled.

A few days later, Max mounted the steps to Rachel's porch, but instead of ringing the doorbell, he swiveled around and looked across the street at his place. He never dreamed he would be living in a house in a small town with red and green lights hanging from it, blazing in the night. He had to admit it gave his home a festive look. The best part of decorating his lawn had been spending time with Rachel and Taylor and even Will and Sam when they'd brought out some of Granny's cookies for them to sample.

"Admiring our handiwork?" Rachel asked from the other end by the swing.

He spun around, making out her form in the shadows. "What are you doing out here?" Moving toward her, he saw her bundled in a blanket.

"I'm giving Taylor some time to finish her schoolwork. I thought if I came out here I wouldn't be tempted to lose my patience with her again today." Scooting over, she made room for him on the swing.

"Bad day?"

"Oh, you could say that. She decided this morning after working an hour she was finished for the day."

"She said that."

"Well, not in those words but she might as well have. Every time I went to do something like pick up Will and Sam from the church I would come back to find her playing on the computer, listening to music. Anything not to work." She twisted toward him, huddled in the warmth offered by the blanket.

The urge to embrace her and warm her inundated him. He locked his arms to his sides.

"She's complaining all I do is make her work. That she can't have any fun. It's close to the winter break for the Tallgrass public schools, and she demanded to know if she was going to get a vacation like all of her friends. She's doing so well with her reading program and today she decided she didn't want to do it anymore. She—"

He laid his fingers over her mouth to still her words, the caress of her lips tingling a path down his length. Quickly, he dropped his hand away. "Shh. It'll work out. Everyone gets tired of what they're doing and needs a break. And that includes you. You've been putting in a lot of time with Taylor. I could help this evening and check on her progress."

"But you came over to help with the food packages."

"Yeah, and I'm going to help, but I thought this project was for everyone. That includes Taylor."

"I can't back down. I told her she had to finish her history before she could do anything else and that includes participating in preparing the boxes."

He framed her face, again acknowledging the danger

of touching her but not able to resist. "Let me take over. When she's through, we'll come into the kitchen to help. Please, Rachel. I would like to do this."

Covering his hands on her, she sighed. "How can I refuse? I don't have the energy to argue and maybe a different approach will work."

"Thanks." He leaned toward her and brushed his lips across hers.

The brief contact bolted such an awareness through him that it robbed him of thought. His mind blanked as he pulled back and stared at Rachel, the glow from her white Christmas lights stressing the flush to her cheeks, the surprise in her eyes.

"Why did you do that?"

"I don't know. It just seemed right at the time."

"With Taylor's paternity up in the air, it probably isn't a smart move."

"Shh. Remember we decided to forget that until after the holidays."

He moved again to sample her lips, slipping his arms around her to bring her up against him. She went into his embrace willingly, returning his kiss with fervor. His heart thudded against his rib cage, and he was sure she felt each beat.

When she finally parted, laying her forehead against his, she murmured, "You know this complicates everything."

"For once, I'm tired of thinking things through first. I want to enjoy your company with no thoughts of the future."

"Seize the moment."

"Why not?"

She inhaled a deep breath. "Well, I must say I feel

much better than when I stomped out here to cool down after fighting with Taylor."

Reluctantly, because he wanted to continue holding her, he released her and rose. "I'll go work with her for a while."

"Those are the sweetest words you could say. Taylor and I need a break from schoolwork. I knew this might be a problem with homeschooling, especially with Taylor's lack of discipline and focus when it comes to academic work. But there are times I have absolutely no patience with my daughter."

"Is she in the dining room?"

"Yep. The boys are in the den. There's no way she can work in there when they're in the room. That's another problem I didn't think through. Keeping them occupied and Taylor focused. I can't be in two places at once, but there are days I need to be."

Max entered the house and headed for the dining room, where he found Taylor staring off into space, her features molded into a frown. She tapped her pencil against her history book.

"Do you need any help?"

Taylor didn't respond. He moved to the table and took a chair near her. She blinked and finally looked at him.

"Need any help?"

She sighed heavily. "Yeah, talk Mom out of making me do this assignment."

"I can't."

"I don't understand why I have to learn history. What good is it? I can't change it. It's about a bunch of people who are dead. Nicholas can study it all he wants, but I don't want to."

"I remember saying that very thing to my parents

when I was growing up. It didn't help. They still insisted I do my best in history. And you know when I quit fighting it, it wasn't so bad."

"I don't care about the Revolutionary War." She chewed on the end of her pencil.

"It's a good way to see how our country started and why. When I see what our ancestors went through so that we could have all our freedoms, it made me appreciate how fortunate I was to live in America."

"Yeah, yeah, I've heard all of that."

"There are some good video series about some of our founding fathers—George Washington, John Adams. Maybe if you watch some of them, you'll get a feel for what those men were like. That might help you understand the times and what they were trying to do. I can say something about that to your mom if you want me to."

Taylor's expression glowed as if she switched on the Christmas lights. "Videos. Yeah. Anything is better than reading this boring stuff about battles."

"That doesn't mean you shouldn't read it."

Her features morphed into a frown again. "Did you know that Mom wants me to read to the old folks at the nursing home?"

"And you don't want to?"

"I can't read out loud to others! I make mistakes. I…"

"Did you tell her?"

"Yes. She told me everyone makes mistakes."

"But to you, reading out loud is a big deal?" His gut fisted at the memory of how he'd felt.

"You bet. That's why I hated school. Some teachers made me read out loud, and I heard some of the kids snicker when I did, so after a while, I refused. I got a detention from one teacher because I wouldn't."

He'd been in the same situation as a child. He remembered dread making him physically sick, especially in one particular class. "I can understand."

"Did you feel that way?"

"Yep."

"Did you ever get over it?"

"To a certain extent but not totally. I ended up practicing at first by myself then later with my mom and younger brother. Once I felt comfortable with them I was better. At least I didn't panic when I was asked to read out loud. I used to break out in a cold sweat."

"You did? So do I."

"If you ever want to read to me, I'd be glad to listen."

"Maybe." She began tapping the pencil against the book again. "What do I tell Mom? I want to volunteer but not for that."

"Ask your mom for other suggestions for volunteering. I think she just wanted you to get a lot of practice reading."

"That's practically all I do. Read science. Read stories for English. Read history. Maybe that's why I like math. Not as much reading."

He pointed toward her history chapter. "What do you have left to do?"

"Mom wants me to summarize what I read. I'm thinking of making a list of battles. That's about all that has happened."

"Let me see. This first section is about Valley Forge. What's important about that?"

"It was cold."

"True. What else?"

"I don't remember. It's been a while since I read it."

"You might want to read a section, write what was important then move on to the next part."

Taylor huffed and slid the book closer to herself.

While Max waited, he heard the front door open and saw Rachel come into the house. She smiled at him and strolled toward the hallway that led to the kitchen. The warmth in her expression spread throughout him. He shouldn't have kissed her earlier—twice. She was right. It complicated everything. He didn't want Rachel to get the wrong idea. His experience with marriage had been bad. Ever since he was a child and struggled with reading, failure didn't sit well with him, and his marriage to Alicia had been a failure. But there was something about Rachel that made him forget all that when he was with her.

Rachel looked toward Will standing on a chair at the counter. "Go easy on stirring the Chex mix."

"It's ready. I did good." He grinned, showing his teeth.

"And I appreciate it. Why don't you help Max and Sam fill the boxes with food."

Will hopped down from the chair and raced into the dining room where Max and Sam were.

"Taylor, can you come in here and put the mix into plastic bags?" Rachel cut her fudge she'd made earlier into pieces.

"Mom, Sam is eating a cookie Granny gave us for the boxes," Taylor said as she came into the kitchen.

Max stuck his head into the doorway. "I'm taking care of it. We're almost through in here."

"Great." Rachel turned toward her daughter. "When

you finish with that, take the boys into the den and make the cards, then we can deliver the packages tonight."

"Max said something about stopping and getting ice cream afterward. Can we?"

"But it's below freezing outside."

"So? I'm still gonna enjoy it."

"Fine." Rachel took the fudge and added the pieces to the goody plates she was preparing for the food boxes.

Ten minutes later, the last items were ready for the gifts to the needy families. While she took the plates into the dining room, Taylor brought in the bags of Chex mix.

"Let's go make the cards," her daughter said, corralling her two younger brothers toward the den.

"This is it." Rachel placed the goodies onto the top of the items in each box.

Max followed behind her and set the plastic bags alongside the plate and closed up the top flaps.

At the last one she noticed an envelope tucked down inside the cartons. "What's this?" She slipped it out and held it up.

"Uh…" Max busied himself sticking one lid under the other to keep it down.

"Max?"

"Okay, it's just a little money to help them get what else they need for Christmas." He looked her right in the eyes. "If you can make up these gift boxes for the families, I can donate some money." A challenge rang in his voice.

"I think that's wonderful. Several of the families go to my church, and I know they could use any help they get."

"Good because I've enjoyed doing this."

She shifted toward him, not realizing he was so close behind her. She bumped into him and his hands came out to steady her. His fingers on her arms, he tugged her nearer. He dipped his head toward her, the scent of his peppermint toothpaste teasing her senses, the feel of his fingers on her skin searing into her.

"I'm glad you're having fun." The sound of her voice barely carried, a breathless quality to it.

"Thanks for including me in this—family activity."

His emphasis on the word *family* should have sent alarm bells clanging in her mind, but she liked the picture that formed in her thoughts. She wanted him to kiss her again. That did make her pause. Everything was moving so fast with Max. Was it because he could be Taylor's natural father? Was it because her boys needed a man around? Those weren't good reasons to pursue a relationship—not in the long run.

"I told you I would show you what the holidays mean to me. It's helping others. Having family around. Celebrating the birth of Christ."

He grinned. "Your concept of Christmas is so much nicer than Mr. Olson's." He cupped her face. "Did I tell you he asked me where my snowman was?"

"No, what did you tell him?"

"I told him it was too hot for the snowman on the street. The glare from all the lights melted him."

"Oh, that's a good one."

"I don't know. I don't think he appreciated the look I gave him. He didn't stay long but hurried down the street." His palms slid back until his fingers threaded their way through her hair.

She was the one who wanted to melt at his caress. Her anticipation heightened with every second, his mouth inching closer to hers.

"We're ready to…"

Rachel leaped back at the same time as Max did. They both swung around and faced Taylor coming into the room with her brothers right behind her. Her daughter's eyes grew round for a few seconds, then her mouth curled up in a huge smile.

"Are you two ready, or do you want us to go back in the den and make more cards?"

The heat from her blush singed Rachel's cheeks. "No, we should go." Was that her voice that squeaked?

"Yeah, it's getting late." Max hefted a box. "Where do I take this?"

"In the back of my SUV. It should hold these. Will and Sam, you two bring the cards."

Fifteen minutes later, Rachel drove down the first street where they were making a delivery. "Okay, Taylor, you know what to do. It looks like the Wilsons are home."

Her daughter climbed from the car parked on the street and grabbed a box from the back, then crossed several yards to the house two down.

"What's she doing?" Max craned his neck to get a good look.

"She'll ring the bell then run. We don't want them to know who left them a box. Once a family caught Taylor before she could get away. They invited us in and gushed over what we'd brought. I'd rather the gift be from a secret friend. It's not the same." As Taylor raced for the SUV, she added, "She enjoys this part the most."

Taylor wrenched open the door and dived into the car. Rachel sped away as the front door opened at the Wilsons' place. Will and Sam giggled.

"You fooled them, sissy." Sam gave Taylor a high five.

Max threw Taylor a glance. "Interesting technique. Drive-by gift giving."

"It's a Howard tradition. Just wait until you see some of our others." Rachel turned the corner on to the street of the second stop.

"Can't wait. What are you going to do? Commando caroling?"

Chapter Eleven

The next afternoon, Taylor sat in the dining room, working on her reading. Suddenly, she stopped in midsentence and peered at Rachel. "I don't want to read to the people at the nursing home. I can't. I'm not ready. I don't know if I ever will be. I'd rather practice with you or even Max. He understands. Did you know he had trouble with reading when he was a kid?"

"You like him?" She was almost afraid to ask the question because she didn't want to feel as if this was a competition between her and Max over Taylor. But if he was her father, it could turn into that. Taylor was her daughter no matter what a test said.

"Yes. We've talked about some of the things he did to learn to read better. He's a doctor. If he can do it, I can, too. I don't want to be dumb."

"You aren't dumb, honey." Rachel put her arms around her daughter and hugged her. "I've noticed you're working hard at reading. I've seen a big improvement in the last month."

"Max got me to thinking when he said commando caroling. What if we sing for them? We could start in the recreation room for the ones who can come there and then go to the rooms of the ones who can't. We could get Aunt Jordan, Uncle Zachary, Nana and whoever else in the family that wants to do it."

"That sounds great. After we finish here, you can make some calls and see who wants to participate."

"I'm sure Max will. He told me he likes to sing."

"You two talk a lot."

"Yeah, I usually see him when I go to Dr. Reynolds's science class. In fact, Max is thinking of offering a class for others in the homeschooling program on Saturday after the New Year. Something to do with the environment. If he does, I'd like to do that."

Max would be here in Tallgrass one way or another even if he wasn't Taylor's father. But he was so positive he was. She needed to decide what she was going to do when they found out for sure in a couple of weeks.

"Are you interested in the environment?" Rachel hooked her hair behind her ears.

"In Sunday-school class we've been talking about being caretakers of what God has given us. That got me to thinking. I want to do my part."

"You don't have to wait until Max's class. You could start now. Maybe come up with ways this family can be green. What do you think?"

"I like that. I could do some research about what a family can do."

"That would be a great project. We could work together, get things that Will and Sam can do, too."

"I can ask Max, too. The reason he said something about an environment class is because he's interested in it. He's been doing a lot of reading on it. Maybe he can share some of it with me. Do you think he would?" Excitement lit Taylor's face.

Her daughter's expression was contagious, and Rachel had Max to thank for it. "Yes, I'm sure he would."

Taylor cocked her head to the side. "You like him, too."

It wasn't a question, but Rachel murmured, "Yes," anyway. She realized *like* was too mild a word to describe the feelings she was developing toward Max. And that thought panicked her. Max was here for Taylor, not her and certainly not to have a relationship with a woman who would only be interested in marriage. On a number of occasions he'd talked about his previous marriage and how he didn't want to repeat that mistake.

"I saw you two the other night. It looked like you were gonna kiss and you're not wearing your wedding ring anymore."

"How do you feel about me taking it off?"

Taylor's teeth dug into her lower lip as she stared at a spot behind Rachel. "I miss Dad a lot. But..."

Her daughter's voice came to a grinding halt, and she dropped her head as though to shield her expression from Rachel. "But what, hon?"

"Dad never had much time for me. He was always working. Now, it's too late for him to spend any time with me. I was so angry when he died. Now, I'm just sad."

"Baby, I'm so sorry. He was doing what he thought he should—helping his patients, providing for his family. I think he always thought he would have the time later. And later never came."

"Pastor John says we need to live in the present."

"Yeah, I guess so. We don't know what the future holds for us."

"So, yes, I'm fine with you taking off your wedding ring. I know you loved Dad."

"I won't forget him. I loved him very much."

Taylor's eyes gleamed with unshed tears. "I know and so did I." She threw her arms around Rachel and squeezed hard. "I love you, Mom. I didn't tell Dad enough."

"I love you, honey." *And I'm falling in love with Max.*

"That was awesome, everyone. I think we're ready for tomorrow." Taylor stood in front of the caroling group in the den. "We'll meet at the nursing home at two. Wear Christmas colors. Aunt Jordan, you'll have the cookies made for us to hand out?"

"Yep. Zachary and Nicholas are helping me tonight when we go home." Jordan settled her hand on her son's shoulder while Zachary pressed her against his side.

"Great. Granny, you'll have the fudge?"

While her grandmother answered yes, Rachel had to keep her mouth from dropping open at Taylor's take-charge attitude. She'd never done that before.

"Mom, how about the Chex mix?"

"Already have it done and ready to go."

"Max, hot chocolate?"

"I'll have it."

Taylor rotated toward her grandmother. "Then that leaves you, Nana, and Dr. Reynolds."

Rachel's mom took Kevin's hand and peered at him. "We've ordered a big cake. We'll pick it up right before we come."

"Thanks, you all. I think the people at the nursing home will enjoy this."

"Bertha said everyone was excited about us coming." Granny grabbed Doug's arm, and he helped her to her feet.

"See you tomorrow then," Taylor said as Ashley came up to her.

"Mom will pick you up at twelve so we can go decorate the recreation room beforehand."

"She's done a good job," Max whispered in Rachel's ear.

His warm breath tickled her neck, and she shivered, a pleasant sensation spreading through her. "Yes, she has. She even called the director of the nursing home to set this up. I'm still amazed at all she's done. In the past she's been a follower, not a leader. This is new for her." Had Max somehow influenced this change in Taylor? Had homeschooling and working on her reading helped Taylor to believe in herself?

"She mentioned to me why she chose to do this was because Bertha was a friend of Granny's. She wanted to do something for her."

"She went to my church until she got sick and had to go into a nursing home. Granny goes to visit Bertha at least once a week." When she saw Taylor take Sam and Will and lead them out of the den, she added, "She's even working with Sam and Will on *Jingle Bells.*"

Taylor stopped in the hallway, swung around and hurried back into the den. Pausing a few feet from Rachel, her daughter motioned to Max.

"Excuse me a sec."

Max's large frame, his back to Rachel, blocked her view of Taylor. They were up to something. After getting off the phone with the nursing home the day before, Taylor kept watching for Max to come home from work, and then when he did, she disappeared across the street for half an hour with a list in her hand.

The feeling she was suddenly being left out of her daughter's life flooded her. Would this be what happened if Max was Taylor's natural father and told Taylor who he was? Her daughter was growing up and would soon have her own life, but she wasn't ready to let her go.

"Are you all right, Rachel?" Jordan approached and took her over to the side away from everyone.

"Sure. Why wouldn't I be?"

"Oh, I don't know. Maybe because you see Max with Taylor and you realize he's becoming important to your daughter."

"Am I that obvious?"

"Only because I know what's going on. I'm sure Mom and Granny don't know a thing. You know they're rooting for you to get together with Max?"

"Yeah, Granny hasn't been too subtle about trying to match me with Max. The other evening she caught me leaving Max's house and asked us to deliver her goodies she baked for the neighbors because she wasn't up to the walk. When Max agreed, she practically danced a jig."

"Back up a sec. You leaving his house? What were you doing there?"

"Returning some reading material Taylor borrowed on the environment." She even took some time to admire the small Christmas tree that Max had put up with brand-new ornaments just out of the box.

"Why didn't she?"

"She was on the phone about the program at the nursing home and asked me." The memory of walking with Max up and down the street, the air laced with the scent of wood burning, the night sky clear with a few stars out, the crispness adding to the atmosphere, pulled her gaze away from her sister and toward Max. The intent look on his face as he talked with Taylor was suddenly switched to her. Her breath caught in her throat, and she had to force deep inhalations into her lungs to keep from getting lightheaded.

"I think you two were had not only by Granny but Taylor, too. Frankly, I don't know why they are wasting their time. It's clear to anyone who is around you all that you don't need any nudging."

"He's a friend."

One of Jordan's eyebrows rose. "Is that what he is to you? What happens if he's Taylor's biological father? What are you gonna do then?"

Rachel chewed on her bottom lip. "I don't know. He has implied several times he doesn't want to get married."

The corners of Jordan's mouth twitched. "Marriage? I didn't say anything about marriage, but it's obvious you've been thinking about it."

"Because that's the only way I could be with a man and I couldn't marry without loving him and him loving me."

"Not even for Taylor?"

"No, because in five or six years she'll be gone, then what will I have?"

"Jordan, we need to get home to bake the cookies," Zachary said at the doorway.

"Okay, just a sec." Her sister shifted her attention back to Rachel. "I'll pray for you, Max and Taylor." She hugged Rachel. "The Lord knows what He's doing."

"I hope so because I'm beginning to think I don't." *I love a man who doesn't want to get married. And if all of sudden he did, what would be his real motive?*

"We'll find our own way out. See you tomorrow." Jordan left with her husband, Nicholas and Ashley.

Before long Granny, Doug, her mother and Kevin were gone. Taylor hurried from the room, too. Max faced her. The quiet was in stark contrast to the chatter of only moments before. The warmth from all those bodies in the den evaporated and left Rachel chilled. She folded her arms across her chest.

He finally broke the silence with, "Only a few days to Christmas."

"What were you and Taylor talking about?"

"Tomorrow."

"What?"

He grinned, laugh lines at the corners of his eyes deepening. "It's a secret. You'll have to wait until tomorrow to find out."

"Why?"

"Because I promised Taylor I wouldn't say anything. It's something she wanted to do and I told her I would help her with it."

She didn't know what to say to that. She frowned.

His smile vanished. "It has nothing to do with why I'm here. Trust me, Rachel. I won't undermine you. I need to go home. Good night."

Before she could move forward, Max strode out into the hallway. She rushed to catch him. "Wait, Max."

At the front door, his hand on the knob, he stopped, but he kept his back to her.

"I know you wouldn't, Max. I'm sorry if that's what you thought. I'm not big on surprises, especially lately."

He peered over his shoulder at her. "This surprise is a good thing. I promise you."

"Fine. Not another word about it."

Sounds came from the kitchen. Will, Sam and Taylor sang *Jingle Bells,* the boys shouting more than singing.

Rachel looked back toward the doorway into the

kitchen, then stepped to Max and stood on her tiptoes to give him a kiss on his cheek. "I hope the people at the nursing home are ready for this. See you tomorrow."

For a second, a bewildered expression widened his eyes slightly before his features settled into a neutral countenance. He nodded. "Tomorrow."

The weakness in her legs forced Rachel to hold on to the door frame as she watched him walk away. Why had she kissed him? What had she been thinking? She hadn't. All she'd thought about was that she didn't want him to leave upset.

Lord, I know You have this all figured out. Could You please clue me in? I feel so confused.

In the recreation room at the nursing home, Rachel bit on the end of her thumbnail. Near her, an old man in his eighties grumbled to the woman next to him about having to wait. Everyone was here except Max. Where was he? Taylor refused to start until he arrived. Did this have anything to do with the surprise he and her daughter had cooked up?

A commotion at the door drew her attention. In walked Max, dressed in a Santa suit carrying a bag over his shoulder.

"Ho! Ho! Ho!"

Will and Sam squealed and clapped, then rushed toward Max. He stooped down to talk to both of them, dug around in his bag and pulled out two wrapped presents for them. Her sons tore into the gifts, paper tossed to the floor. Their eyes lit up like a Christmas tree when they saw the semitrucks.

"Thanks, Santa." Sam hugged the toy to his chest.

"Yeah," Will added.

Taylor stepped toward Max. "I'm so glad you could

come, Santa. We have some special guests here." She gestured toward the twenty-five senior citizens sitting around in a half circle, some in wheelchairs.

"Ho. Ho. Ho. So I see, and I've got some special presents for them."

Several of the seniors perked up and sat straighter. The eighty-year-old man continued to grumble under his breath he was too old for a visit from Santa. The woman next to him told him to hush up. The man snapped his mouth closed and glared at a spot on the floor by his feet. Rachel clamped her lips together to keep from smiling at the exchange.

Max ambled toward the front of the room. "What do you all want first? Presents or caroling?"

Everyone but the grumpy old man shouted, "Presents."

"Well, let me see what I have in here." Max rummaged in his bag and withdrew one. "This says Bertha on it."

"Me." Granny's friend raised her arm, waving.

Max approached her and made a big production out of giving her the gift, then went back to his bag for the next one. As people opened their surprises, Max passed out all the presents. A few gasps and ahs filled the room. Rachel panned the faces of the seniors and marveled at the joy in their expressions.

She sidled toward her daughter. "Did you have anything to do with this?"

Taylor beamed. "Yes. The director told me quite a few of the seniors won't have much for Christmas. I wanted to do something for them. I found out what they needed or wanted and tried to get it."

"You should have said something to me. I'd have helped."

"I didn't need to. You had the care packages for those families. I happened to say something to Max and he loved the idea. He wanted to help me."

What her daughter did was wonderful, but a seed of jealousy planted itself in Rachel's heart. She felt as if Max was moving in on her territory, and she didn't like that she was upset by it. "How did you buy all this?"

"I used the money I was saving for an iPod, and Max helped with the rest. He, Nana and me went to the store and got everything."

"That evening you went to Mom's?"

Taylor nodded, pleased with herself. "I wanted it to be a surprise, and I really don't want people to know that I did it. Those gifts are from Santa if anyone asked."

Suddenly her daughter sounded older than she was as though she'd grown up overnight. "What you did was great, honey. All you have to do is look at their faces to see the happiness you've brought to them."

"That's my gift. It was so much fun buying for them. Now I see why you like doing those care boxes every year."

As Taylor moved toward the front of the room, Rachel swung her attention to Max. A room separated them, but the other people for a moment faded from her consciousness as she stared at him. His smile encompassed his whole face from the gleam in his gaze to the deep crinkles at the sides of his eyes to the dimples that appeared in his cheeks. Joy infused her whole being.

This man was good for her daughter whether he was Taylor's natural father or not. In that moment, she knew what she would do when they got the results from the DNA testing. She wouldn't stand in his way of becoming part of Taylor's life even though being around him constantly would be difficult for her because she loved him and wanted more than what he was willing to offer.

"Taylor wants to take our caroling on the road." Rachel sat on the porch swing later that evening, cupping a mug of hot chocolate that Max had fixed from scratch in her hands.

"I know. She mentioned it earlier. I told her I draw the line at wearing a Santa suit again. It was hot. Did you see the sweat pop out on my forehead?" The stream of light from the living room illuminated Max's teasing expression.

"I have a feeling if Taylor asked you to again you would. I think you're putty in her hands."

"Shh. Don't say that too loud. Am I that obvious?"

"Yep." Rachel sipped her drink, remembering the time and care Max had taken in preparing the hot chocolate just right. Although it was near freezing, Max's nearness created a warmth in her that went all the way to her toes.

"I can't believe tomorrow is Christmas Eve, and I'm not working on Christmas Eve or Christmas. I have for so many years I'm not sure what to do with the time."

"You're coming to my house for dinner with the whole family. After that you might need to recover. It's an experience, possibly not worth repeating, to be around two four-year-olds at Christmas."

"Should I bring anything?"

"Only a secret Santa gift."

"Secret Santa?" He took a sip of his hot chocolate, relaxing back, his arm brushing up against hers.

"It's a game we play every year. We each make a present, then on Christmas all draw numbers. The person with number one will choose a present first. If there's a gift you like that someone else already has opened, you can take it away from that person if it's your turn. Some people will. Some won't. It can get pretty ruthless but always in a fun way."

"I have to make a present! When were you going to tell me?"

"I'm sorry. I forgot with all that's been going on this month."

"And I can't go out and buy anything?" Panic laced his voice.

She shook her head.

"You did this on purpose," he said in a mockingly stern tone. "You've probably had your gift done ages ago."

"Yep. I don't like to wait until the last minute."

"And you think I do?"

"Tell you what. I've got something I can give you to use."

He thrust his shoulders back. "Nope. I'll come up with something." He swallowed the last of his drink and rose. "Which means I need to go and start working on what I'm bringing."

She didn't want him to leave. "You can't stay for a while? Taylor is spending the night at Ashley's. The boys are in bed early for a change. I'm not going to know what to do with myself."

"You finished your Christmas quilt?"

"Done."

"You've wrapped all your presents?"

"Done."

"Your Christmas cards?"

"Mailed two weeks ago."

"And I know your house has been decorated for a month."

"So, what should I do with this unexpected free time?" There was a part of her that was stunned she was being so bold, but since he had come into her life, she realized she had been lonely since Lawrence's death. Max filled an empty place in her heart. She wished she did in his. That was the problem. His was closed off from others. He was scared to care too deeply for another. He'd seen so much of how precarious life was in his profession with trauma situations.

"I could build a fire and we could sit in front of it."

Rachel inhaled a deep breath. The scent of others who'd done that spiced the air. "I don't very often anymore. That would be nice." She'd stopped doing it when Lawrence died. He'd always been the one who'd wanted a fire going. She needed to build new memories.

Max rose and held out his hand to her. She took it, and he tugged her up against him. Tilting her face up to his, she ran her finger along his jawline, the stubble from a day's growth of beard rough beneath her pad.

A shadow of pain inched into his features. He captured her hand and stilled its movement. "What are we doing?"

"We're going to sit in front of a fire and talk."

"No, this. I don't want us to be just friends. Right this moment I want to kiss you. I want to hold you against me. I want to…" He drew in a ragged breath. "This probably isn't smart until we know what's up about Taylor. I won't walk away from my daughter. I didn't have a choice thirteen years ago, but as far as I'm concerned, I don't have a choice now. She is my flesh and blood. A part of me."

"In the end, what's best for Taylor is the most important thing to be considered."

"And what is that?"

A dash of cold reality struck her in the face. Rachel backed away, her arms falling to her sides. "I don't know. I'm not even sure Taylor knows what is best for her. Your arrival has complicated everything." Made her come out of her comfort zone and acknowledge she needed more than she had.

He stiffened. "So, what you see in me is a complication?"

"I care about you, but to take that any further is a complication."

"I failed at my first marriage and look what happened. Taylor is with you."

"I haven't said anything about marriage, and Taylor being with me isn't a bad thing."

"You're twisting my words around." His words were grounded out between clenched teeth.

"Am I? I know what a good marriage is, and I won't settle for anything less than that if I ever decide to marry again."

"And you shouldn't settle for less."

"You have a lot to offer a woman, but because of Alicia, who you can't seem to forgive, you don't see that. You can decide to either dwell in the past or live in the present. That's your choice. I choose the here and now. I hope my daughter does, too."

"What's that supposed to mean?"

"If the DNA results come back that Taylor is your child, I'll acknowledge what happened to you was a bad deal, but I can't change that and neither can you. I won't let you take Taylor away from me." Rachel sprayed her hand over her heart. "She's my daughter in here, no matter what a test says. My lawyer says I have a good case, and you probably wouldn't get custody, not even partial."

"That'll be for the court to decide, if need be. I'd better go. It's getting late." He spun about on his heel and strode away.

The rigid set to his shoulders and the clenched hands at his sides magnified his anger. She started forward to stop him. Halted in midstep and stayed where she was. What could she say to him? That she would share her daughter with him every other weekend or some type of agreement as if they were a divorced couple? No. She couldn't do that to Taylor.

Chapter Twelve

"I thought Max was joining us for Christmas dinner." Jordan popped a carrot stick into her mouth.

"He's supposed to. Maybe there was a medical emergency." In her kitchen Christmas morning, Rachel stared at the celery she was slicing for the relish dish.

"Or maybe there's something else going on. I also thought he was going with us to church last night. He came alone and sat behind us, then left before I could say hi."

Rachel recalled Max slipping in late in the pew behind her and just as quietly slipped away when the choir finished and the service was over. He'd been there for Taylor. She had to remember her daughter was behind everything he did. She was his focus.

"What's going on? I thought you two were really getting along."

"What's that supposed to mean?" Rachel stacked the celery sticks on the tray and set it in the refrigerator.

"Just exactly what I said." Jordan moved closer, glanced over her shoulder then lowered her voice and said, "If you two married that would solve a lot of problems."

"We don't know if he's Taylor's father. Besides, marrying because of a child isn't a good enough reason and, believe me, Max feels strongly about that."

Jordan's eyebrows lifted. "Oh, he does? So you've talked to him about marriage."

"Well, no, not exactly. But I know his views on marriage. He was burned by his wife. Look what she did by putting their child up for adoption without him knowing."

"What I want to know is what do you want?"

"I want you and Granny to stop trying to match us up."

Jordan waved her hand. "Besides that."

"Ha! I knew you two wouldn't let it go."

"You're avoiding the question."

"I never thought I wanted to get married again, either. Now I know I do." Rachel held up her palm to stop Jordan from saying anything. "But only if the man loves me and wants to be with *me* the rest of his life. I won't settle for anything less."

"And you don't think Max would ever feel that way?"

"How would I ever know if Taylor turns out to be his daughter?"

"By trusting yourself—God."

"That's easy for you to say. You aren't in this situation."

"You don't trust the Lord to show you the right way?"

"It's more complicated than that." Rachel wiped down the counter. Her feelings concerning Max had developed like an erupting volcano—suddenly and explosively. Her feelings for Lawrence had been formed slowly over time. They snuck up on her, whereas with Max, she felt overwhelmed with emotions from the very beginning.

The doorbell chimed, and Taylor shouted, "I'll get it."

"That must be Mom and Kevin. I'm glad he decided to come." Rachel draped the washcloth over the middle section of the double sink.

"Yeah, they're getting serious. It's about time. Do you think Granny moving out prompted this?"

Rachel leaned back against the counter, grasping its edge on both sides of her. "I think it's made her reassess her life. No one wants to be left alone."

"Are you speaking about yourself?"

"Taylor will be leaving in five or six years. The boys will follow nine or ten years after that. I'll be younger than Mom is now."

"This is new. You have been thinking about it."

"Lately."

"Ever since Max came to town. Interesting."

Taylor appeared in the entrance from the hallway. "Mom, Max is here and Granny and Doug came right behind him. When is Nana gonna get here so we can open presents?"

"I don't know. Why don't you give her a call?"

"I'll just go to her house. She might need help with the gifts." Taylor whirled around and rushed down the hall.

"Where's Taylor racing off to?" Max filled the entrance not seconds after Taylor left.

Rachel's pulse pounded through her veins. The conversation with her sister made her realize how much she was falling for this man. A man who was only concerned about his daughter. A man who didn't believe in marriage—like she did. "To get Mom. Nothing can start until she comes."

"Oh, I see why she's in a hurry."

"I'm gonna go see if Granny and Doug need any help." Jordan squeezed past Max still in the doorway.

Could she flee, too? The tension in the room surrounded Rachel as though it were a palpable force. Her grip on the counter's edge strengthened until her fingers hurt. "I didn't think you would come."

"Do you want me to leave?"

"No." *Why can't their situation be simple? Girl meets boy. Girl falls in love with boy. Girl lives happily ever after married to boy.* "It's just the last time we talked we didn't part on good terms."

"I wouldn't miss this first Christmas with—here in Tallgrass."

The fleeting haunted look that flickered in and out of his eyes swelled her chest with feelings she wanted to deny. But she couldn't. She loved him and he didn't feel that way toward her. "I hope you enjoy yourself." She turned, facing the sink and grabbing the washcloth. With her focus on the already cleaned counter, she began wiping it down again. Anything to hide the fact her hands shook, her heart was breaking.

A commotion in the foyer drifted to her.

"It looks like your mom is here."

The feel of his look on her burned through her defenses. "Yeah, the festivities can begin. Let them know I'll be in there in a minute."

A long pause, then Max said in a tone that sounded prickly like pine needles on a Christmas tree, "I'll do that."

Squeezing her eyes closed, she listened to him head down the hall toward the den. Happy voices echoed through the house. Laughter and shouts of joy followed. She needed to go in there and act as though she were fine. She didn't know if she could. Not since Lawrence's sudden death had she experienced such helplessness.

Lord, please help me. What do I do?

With the Christmas dinner eaten and the dishes done, Rachel finally sat in the den near the roaring fire. The heat warmed her chilled body. She needed an answer to what to do about Max. None came to mind. All the presents had been opened hours ago. The whole day had been filled with merriment and cheer, but nothing seemed to touch the coldness that embedded itself deep in her bones.

Soon she and Max would find out if Taylor was really his daughter, but lately in her heart she knew he was. Glimpses of them together confirmed it. The way she pressed her lips together when she was thinking. Max did, too. The tilt of his head reminded Rachel of Taylor when she was questioning something—usually her about something her daughter didn't want to do.

"It's time for secret Santa." Jordan stood in the middle of the room. "For the newcomers, the rule is you can steal a present from someone else, but a gift can only be stolen twice then it's dead. No one else can take it." Holding a bag with numbers in it, her sister started with Granny. "Whoever gets one goes first. And remember, if you want someone else's present don't be shy. Steal it. This is the only time it's okay to do that."

"I got one," her mother said, waving the piece of paper. She rose and walked to the group of wrapped boxes. After shaking a few, she selected a gift and opened it. Fudge from Granny.

Rachel looked at her number. Nine. By the time it was her turn five presents had been revealed. The one she wanted was a loaf of banana nut bread made by Sam with

Granny's help. She took it from Zachary. He frowned and grumbled but picked another gift to unwrap—a quilt showing different winter scenes that Rachel had made.

The next person, Doug, stole the quilt away from Zachary. More grumbles sounded and he selected a third package—a dinner cooked and catered by Max.

"Finally, a gift I can sink my teeth into." Zachary pumped the air. "And no one better take this one."

Max was next and wandered around the room, inspecting each gift. He paused in front of her, took the bread, saying, "Smells great," but gave it back to Rachel, his gaze linking with hers for a long few seconds before he moved on.

She inhaled deeply. Her heart thumped against her chest.

Max stopped in front of Doug and grabbed the quilt that the older man tried to hide. "I believe this means it's dead. No one can take it from me."

Rachel peered at him as he sat, cradling the gift in his arms.

Taylor was the last person to pick a present. She headed straight for Rachel and snatched the bread. "This is my favorite."

That left Rachel to put an end to the game by opening the last one under the tree. Everyone encouraged her to do that. She couldn't. Instead she made a beeline for Zachary. There was no doubt what she wanted. She laid her palm out flat. "I'll take the dinner."

Zachary glared at her and begrudgingly gave it to her. "The only way I won't get a gift stolen from me is to take the last one." He plucked it up and tore into it. When he saw it, he smiled from ear to ear. "I got the best one of all. A Christmas story by my son."

While Jordan and Granny asked for Zachary to read it

out loud, Rachel folded the piece of paper into her hand. A dinner with Max or at least one he prepared for her. She probably wouldn't have done it if he hadn't taken her quilt. The gesture gave her courage. A ray of hope. Was this the sign telling her what to do?

Rachel signed for the certified envelope three days after Christmas. When the mailman left, she hurried to her bedroom and closed the door, locking it. Taylor was working in the kitchen, complaining she had to work a few hours when it was winter vacation for everyone else. Rachel didn't want her daughter to disturb her while she read the DNA test results. Sinking onto her bed, her hands trembling so much she could hardly hold the letter, she laid it in her lap and stared at it. Oklahoma Diagnostic Lab. The bold lettering taunted her. *Open me.*

If Taylor was Max's daughter, she'd be tied to him forever. How was she going to be able to do that loving him the way she did and he not returning those feelings?

She started to rip into it when the phone rang. She snatched it up before Taylor answered it. "Hello." Even that one word shook with her stress.

"Rachel, I got the DNA results." Not a hint of what the results were sounded in Max's husky, bass voice.

"I did, too." She tore the end of the envelope.

"Have you read it yet?"

"No. You?"

"Yes. Read it. I'll wait."

She didn't need to because she could hear it suddenly in his voice. Relief. Confirmation, finally. "Just a minute." Placing the phone on the bedside table, she sucked in a fortifying breath and slid her finger in the slit to open it. She held the paper in both hands, her whole body quaking.

He was Taylor's biological father. Her heart plummeted into her stomach. What was she going to do?

"Rachel."

Max's voice came to her from the receiver. She picked it up. "I'm here."

"We need to talk."

"When?"

"Soon."

"I'll have Jordan come get the kids and have them spend the night at the ranch. We can talk this evening." Which only gave her a few hours to decide what to do.

"Fine. I'll be over at seven. Okay?"

"Yeah, I'll see you then." She quickly hung up before she dropped the phone.

Clasping her hands together, she stared at a spot on her floor, a flaw in the hardwood.

You can always refuse him access to Taylor, a little voice needled her.

She couldn't. She didn't know how she could keep this from Taylor because if she did and her daughter discovered she had, that could destroy their relationship. She couldn't take that chance. Besides, Max could take her to court and then Taylor would definitely know what was going on. No, her daughter needed to find out from her.

But not before she knew Max's intentions now that it was confirmed by the DNA test.

Pounding at her door jerked her head up. "Mom." The knob rattled. "Why's the door locked?"

Rachel shoved to her feet and let Taylor into the bedroom. "Can't I have a few minutes of quiet time?"

"Fine. But Sam and Will have found the empty rolls of wrapping paper and are using them as swords."

A crash alerted Rachel that one had connected with something fragile. She hurried down the hall toward the den, glad for once for a distraction.

Right before she went into the room, Taylor shouted from the other end of the corridor, "Can I stop today? I've finished the page of math problems."

"Yes. Yes." She turned into the den and saw the lamp she and Lawrence had bought their first Christmas, smashed on the floor.

She came to a halt. Tears swamped her, blurring her vision. She felt like that lamp, shattered into a hundred pieces.

Max paced his den floor. In a few minutes, he needed to go over to see Rachel about what they were going to do concerning Taylor. What he'd started two months before when he'd come to Tallgrass was finally coming to an end. Taylor would know the truth soon.

But what was he going to do about their relationship in the future? Not his and Taylor's—that he knew what he was going to do—but his and Rachel's.

He hadn't thought he would do this, but the most logical thing for him to do was marry Rachel. Then he would truly be a part of Taylor's family. He cared deeply for Rachel, and he could be a good father to Will and Sam.

It could work out for everyone. With his decision made, he left his house to go across the street to Rachel's.

"Come in. Everyone is gone." Rachel stepped to the side and let Max into her house that evening precisely at seven o'clock. "We'll talk in here." She gestured toward the living room, purposely choosing the more formal setting for their conversation.

To further distance herself from him, she took a chair across from him on the couch. She'd talked again with her lawyer today, and he'd assured her she stood on firm grounds and was in a better position than Max in this case. And yet, that didn't stop her from feeling as though Max had a right to spend time with Taylor. How could she totally ignore that he was her daughter's biological father and the fact Taylor was taken away from him through no fault of his?

"I guess the first question to ask is where do we go from here?" Max sat on the edge of the sofa, his legs spread apart, his elbows on his thighs, his hands clasped together. The only indication of his stress was in his white knuckles.

"We talk to Taylor and let her know you're her biological father."

Some of his tension faded, his grip loosening, color flooding back into his fingers. "When?"

"I'll see if Mom or Granny can watch the boys tomorrow evening. We'll tell her then."

"I want to tell her everything. Nothing held back. She deserves that."

"Yes."

"I want to be in her life, be here for her. I want her to know that."

"What's that mean to you? I won't give up custody of Taylor. She needs to know I love her no matter what a test says."

"I agree. Taylor comes first in whatever we do." He dropped his gaze away for a long moment, tension seeping back into his frame. When he reestablished eye contact with her, she could tell from his expression he'd come to a decision. "I've been thinking long and hard about this—about a way this could work with no one getting hurt." He paused, then rushed on. "We could get married. Be a family."

His proposal stole her breath, her thoughts. All she could do was stare at him.

The solution would be perfect if only he loved her. "Have you forgiven Alicia for what she did?" She finally asked the only question that came into her mind.

He clamped his mouth together, the hard line of his jaw announcing his answer without him saying a word. "No, I'm trying. But she took so much from me."

"So, your feelings about marriage are still the same? I can't marry anyone who doesn't believe in it. I can't marry anyone who doesn't love me. I want to be the reason a man wants to marry me, not my daughter. It wouldn't work, and you said so yourself you won't go through that kind of marriage again."

"You aren't anything like Alicia. There is no comparison." The savage twist to his words accentuated the anger he still held close to his heart.

"I love you. Do you love me?"

"I—" His hesitation spoke volumes.

"No, I won't do that to myself."

She wanted—deserved—a man who could answer without a second thought. "I won't keep you away from Taylor, but I won't put my children through a marriage that's a sham. There's more to consider here than just Taylor." *Me. My breaking heart.* She rose and nearly sank back down from the weakness that attacked her legs.

He came to his feet, a bleak look on his face. "I'm sorry."

"I'll see you tomorrow evening at the same time."

She had to cut him off, not wanting to hear his excuses of why he couldn't love her for herself, not the fact she was Taylor's mother. She had to mean more to a man than that. She started for the foyer, desperately needing to be alone. "Taylor will dictate how much you're in her life. That's the way it has to be. I won't force my daughter into something she doesn't want."

He didn't say anything but strode toward the door and thrust it open. "Fine, Taylor will always come first. See you tomorrow evening."

Tears crammed her throat, but she wouldn't cry in front of him. *Taylor will always come first.* His clipped words cut through the numb feeling descending. And that was why she would have to find a way to distance herself from Max, harden her heart to him, or she wasn't sure how she would make it through the days to come.

The past few days had left Max exhausted, working long hours while trying to deal with the confirmation he was really Taylor's father. He had known it, but it was good to have it proved with the DNA test.

As he approached Rachel's house, his gut churned as though a caustic poison had eaten holes in it. He'd taken antacids all day but nothing calmed his stomach. What if Taylor rejected him? What if the past two months had meant nothing?

Why hadn't Rachel agreed to marry him? He cared about her. He love... The thought slammed him to a halt.

The anguish he'd seen in Rachel's face yesterday evening when she'd told him she loved him nipped at his composure and roiled through him like a tsunami. He couldn't dwell on that right now. One thing at a time. Moving forward, he pushed it back into the dark recesses of his mind only to be shoved forward again when Rachel answered the door.

The haunted look in her eyes ripped his composure to shreds. He'd hurt her badly and hadn't wanted to. He'd thought asking her to marry him could be a solution to the situation, but now he realized it hadn't been. It had only worsened the problem, and now she wouldn't believe him if he suddenly declared his love.

"She's in the den reading a novel. When I went in there to tell her you were coming over, I was shocked to see her reading for pleasure. The first time I've seen that."

"What's she reading?" he asked to delay what needed to be done. He rubbed his sweaty palms against his jeans.

"A young adult book she got when Jordan took Nicholas to the library today. My daughter informed me she applied for a library card. That was shock number two."

And what would shock number three be? Taylor's reaction to the news he was her father? "A bookstore is one of my favorite places. I'll have to take her to one soon."

"Maybe we could go together..." Rachel shook her head. "Sorry, that would be a nice outing for you two."

"Rachel, you'll always be welcome to come. You've been more than generous to me."

She moved close and lowered her voice. "Because it's the right thing to do. Taylor deserves to have a say in this."

He released a trapped breath. "Yes, and I want to get this over with." *Before I back out of telling Taylor who I am.* "In all the things I've had to deal with, this will be one of the most difficult." *Next to having to tell you who I am.*

"I have to admit it's on my top-ten list of hard things to do."

"After you."

Rachel led the way to the den. He hung back for a few seconds, trying to gather the courage to do what he'd wanted to do since he'd discovered he had a child.

Inside the entrance into the room Max stopped and scanned the area, full of Christmas with an eight-foot, live pine tree in the corner, still decorated with ornaments that Rachel had for years. Whereas his small one had all brand-new ones on it, a perfect symbol of his life at the moment. Brand-new with possibilities.

Curled up on the sofa, Taylor glanced up from reading her book. "Mom said you were coming over. What's up?"

"We have something to talk to you about." The solemn tone in his voice wasn't exactly the way he'd wanted to do it. He'd made it sound like some bad news was going to follow. "Actually, something exciting," he added with a smile that quivered at the corners of his mouth as if he'd been forced to hold that pose for a long time.

"Exciting news?" Taylor peered at him then her mother. A grin all the way to the gleam in her green eyes graced her face. "News you want to tell me?" She closed her book and laid it on the table next to her. "I think I know what you two want to share."

"You do?" How? Panic set in until Max noticed she was genuinely smiling.

"Yeah, I've seen you all together. Talking—" Taylor paused as if for a dramatic effect "—kissing. You two have finally decided to make it official. You're dating."

Max sank into the chair nearby. This wasn't starting

out great. "I think you've got it mixed up." Although the idea appealed to him a lot.

The gleam in her eyes glinted like the star at the top of the Christmas tree. "You two are engaged?"

Engaged? Words fled his mind. If he and Rachel were engaged, would this be easier?

"Honey, please let Max tell you what he came here for." Rachel gripped the back of the chair he sat in.

"Something's wrong?" Concern replaced Taylor's grin.

"I don't consider it wrong. In fact, I think it is very right." He surged to his feet and paced in front of the couch, tossing his glance toward Taylor. *Lord, if You're listening, please give me the right words.* "I want to tell you a little about myself beyond the fact I struggled to learn to read."

He stopped in front of the coffee table and faced Taylor—his daughter. The thought still brought joy to him. "I was married a long time ago. My wife and I both made some mistakes, but even though I was deployed overseas several times in our marriage, I wanted to work to keep it together. She didn't. While in Bosnia, I received a letter from her and divorce papers to sign."

Taylor opened her mouth to say something but didn't.

With a deep breath, he continued, "I never heard from my wife after that. Everything came through her lawyer. I didn't even know where she moved. But six months ago I got a call from my ex-wife's sister. She needed to see me. She only lived an hour and a half from New York City so I went to see her on the following weekend. I found out Alicia had just died."

"I'm sorry, but—"

"There is a point to this. Her sister gave me some

papers that Alicia had to confirm what she was about
to tell me. You see, my ex-wife was pregnant when she
divorced me. She gave the child up for adoption without
my knowledge. According to her sister, she insisted she
didn't know who the father was. But that wasn't the truth.
I was the father, and she didn't want to be connected to
me in any way."

Her brow furrowed, Taylor glanced at Rachel then
back at Max. "What's that got to do with us?"

"After months of searching, I finally discovered where
my daughter was. Here in Tallgrass." He gulped in a lung
full of air. "It's you, Taylor."

"Me!" Taylor shot to her feet, her arms ramrod
straight at her sides. "No, it's a mistake. I can't…" She
pressed her lips together, glaring from Max to Rachel.
"Tell me it isn't so."

"Honey, it is. We ran a DNA test to make sure."

His daughter's mouth fell open. Tears welled into her
eyes. He took a step toward her. Rachel came around the
chair and toward Taylor.

She held up her hand. "Don't come near me."

Before he could say anything, his daughter fled the
den.

Chapter Thirteen

Max started after Taylor. Rachel blocked his path.

He stared down at her. "I need to explain. I didn't do a good job."

"There was no easy way to tell her. Let me talk to her. Give her time. This is a lot to take in. She didn't go out looking for you. You found her."

"I can't leave it like this."

"You have to." Rachel forced a cold tone into her voice. She wasn't sure what she'd expected—that her daughter would throw her arms around Max and welcome him into her family? She'd known that Taylor didn't adjust well to change and this was a big one. Maybe she'd been wrong in doing it this way. "Time, Max. You don't have a choice."

The sound of a door slamming shut upstairs vibrated through the air. He appeared as though he'd been slapped by the noise. Color leached from his face. "Fine. Talk to her, but please call me afterward. I need to know what's going on with Taylor."

"I will, but don't be surprised if she won't talk to me tonight. You'll have to have patience. Routine is so important to Taylor, and at the moment she feels her whole life has been disrupted."

"She knew she was adopted."

"But finding her birth parents had never been an issue with her. We rarely talked about it and haven't for years. The reality of it has to be a big shock for her."

Rachel walked with Max to the front door and waited until he descended the steps before heading up the staircase to the second floor.

She knocked on her daughter's door. Nothing. She thought about leaving and trying again, but something prompted her to try the knob. Unlocked, she eased into the bedroom. Taylor wasn't on her bed, at her desk or in her overstuffed chair. The closet. Although the door was closed, Rachel knew she was in there.

"Taylor, please talk to me."

"Go away," she screamed.

"Honey, I know you're hurting. I want to help you."

The closet door flew open. Taylor, her hair messy as if she'd run her hands through it repeatedly, filled the entrance. No tears visible in her eyes, only anger. "I'm not a baby. Quit treating me like one. How long have you known Max was my father?" She thumped a fist into her chest. "I'm the last person to discover something important about *me*."

"We only found out yesterday about the DNA results."

"Why didn't you tell me what you were doing? I'm not a baby."

"I didn't want you to worry about something that might not be true." *I did the job for you.*

"So you were protecting me?"

I was protecting me, too. "You had a father who you loved very much. Then all of a sudden to tell you that another man was your father wasn't something I wanted to tell you unless it was one hundred percent true."

Tears flooded her eyes. "Did Dad love me? He never had time for me. He kept putting things off to later and now later is here and he isn't."

Rachel took a step toward Taylor. "Your father loved you. He worked hard to provide a good life for us."

Taylor backed up. "I wanted him. He didn't get to come to my softball games or my school program or…" Raw hurt saturated her voice until she couldn't say another word. Taylor sucked in a shaky breath and moved farther into her closet.

"Honey, I'm so sorry. Why didn't you say anything to me?"

"If Dad didn't want to spend time with me, I didn't want him to feel he had to. He had to because he wanted to."

Rachel wrapped her arms around her daughter. Her feelings mirrored how she felt about Max. He had to want to be with her, not just Taylor, or a marriage would never work in the end. Her own tears surged into her eyes as she held Taylor.

Max rapped on Pastor John's office door, open a few inches to allow Max to see inside. The man looked up from working at his desk and greeted him with a smile.

"Come in. It was nice seeing you Christmas Eve at church."

Max trudged into the room, feeling as though his shoulders were weighted down with his past. "I need some help with something I've been wrestling with."

"Sure. I'm always here to help." Pastor John rose, moved to a sitting area and took a chair.

Max folded his length in the seat across from the minister. "What do you do when you can't seem to get past a betrayal that happened to you?"

"May I ask what happened?"

Max braced himself with a gulp of air then launched into an explanation of what occurred between him and Alicia. "She's dead, but I'm still full of anger at what she did to me. Rachel doesn't think I can move forward without dealing with what Alicia did to me and forgiving her."

"What do you think?"

He remembered the look on Taylor's face as he told her who he was. He recalled the sound of her slamming a door. But mostly he couldn't forget Rachel when she told him she loved him but couldn't settle for anything but a man totally committed to her. And she was totally right. If he couldn't give that to her, they shouldn't get involved. He loved her. But if he couldn't move on from his past, he needed to back away from her—at least as much as he could and still be part of Taylor's life. That was if his daughter wanted him in her life.

"I think I have a mess on my hands. How do I right everything?"

"Ask the Lord for help. He's the only one who can help you. Do I think Rachel is right about forgiveness? Yes. Do I think it's easy to forgive someone, especially when that person did something that really hurt you? No. It will be one of the hardest things you've done. But then the Lord doesn't ask easy things of us."

"Every time I try to forgive Alicia for what she did I get angry again. I think of the thirteen years I've lost with Taylor." Max threaded his fingers together, so tightly pain spread up his arm.

"Will being angry bring those years back?"

"No."

"Is being angry making you happy?"

Max shook his head, his throat closing.

"Look at it this way. What would have happened if Alicia had terminated the pregnancy instead of putting Taylor up for adoption? You would have nothing now. No daughter to love even if she's thirteen. You've got years to enjoy being her father. Years that if Alicia hadn't had Taylor you wouldn't have."

"So, I should count my blessings and forget the other?"

"What you do is up to you. There's a verse in Ephesians that I think says it all. 'And be ye kind one to another, tenderhearted, forgiving one another even as God for Christ's sake hath forgiven you.'"

Max put his hands on the arms of the chair and pushed himself to his feet. "Thanks, Pastor John. You've given me something to think—and pray about."

"My door is open any time you need to talk."

When Max exited the church, he didn't want to get in his car. Restless energy poured through him. He decided he would walk for a while. The park downtown was only a block and a half away.

He pulled the front of his heavy coat together, zipping it up to ward off the bite of the northerly wind. When he reached the park, he found a bench near the playground where several mothers had brought their children. Even one father had two little boys, bundled against the cold, running across the wooden bridge between the jungle gym and the slide. A little girl fell off a swing and began wailing. He started to get up to help, but the child's mother soothed her. After a minute, the girl hopped to her feet as though nothing had happened and raced off to play on a wooden climbing structure.

He'd never had that with Taylor. The anger bubbled to the surface.

But God has given you a gift. Not only Taylor but a woman who is a wonderful mother to your daughter. She has soothed Taylor's tears through the years in his place.

Being around Rachel and her children these past two months, he knew he wanted more. He wanted a family.

I want a wife to share it with. I want Rachel. I love her. No reservations.

That realization really didn't take him by surprise. When he pictured his future, Taylor was in it but so was Rachel.

Yes, the Lord had given him a gift. And if he had to forgive Alicia in order to accept the gift, then he would gladly. He was tired of being alone.

Later that night Max prowled his den, trying to decide what to do next. He had to convince Rachel she was the reason he wanted to get married. Not Taylor.

But he had almost no practice at being romantic. He was much more comfortable in an emergency room patching up a gunshot wound or in a tent in the desert trying to save a bomb victim.

When the doorbell rang, he whirled around toward the foyer. Rachel. Maybe she had news about Taylor. He hadn't talked with either one since last night although he had started to call half a dozen times that day.

The chime sounded again. He hurried to the entry hall and pulled the door open, hoping it was Rachel.

Taylor slouched in the entrance. She lifted her head and gave him a smile that faded quickly. "Can I come in?"

"Of course."

A gust of chilly wind blew into the house along with Taylor. She shivered, hugging her arms to her chest, her shoulders hunched. "I think it's gonna snow."

"Instead of a white Christmas, we'll have a white New Year."

"Maybe." Taylor ambled into the den, staring at the fireplace, minus any warm fire in it. When she pivoted toward him, she rubbed her hands up and down her arms.

"I can start a fire if you want."

"No, that's okay. I can't stay long. Tonight Mom goes to her quilting group at church and I need to babysit Will and Sam."

"Does she know you're here?"

"Yes." Taylor slid her gaze away for a moment then looked back at Max. "Mom and I talked last night and today. I'm okay with everything now."

"Are you, really? You were pretty angry last night."

"Yeah, I know. I was surprised, then I began to remember things about my dad. Things I wish I could have changed. Now I can't."

"What things?" He didn't want to make the same mistakes. He'd made enough already with Taylor and Rachel.

"Dad used to tell me he loved me, that I was his little girl, but we never spent much time together. He worked all the time. I began to feel his patients were more important to him than me. I started going with him to his office on some Saturdays to try to be with him, but he was always working on his notes, stuff he didn't do during the week. Now I can't. He's gone."

The tightness in his throat expanded. He swallowed several times. "I know I can't replace your dad, but I hope we can have a relationship together. The Lord gave me a gift for Christmas—the best present ever. You."

A sheen of tears glittered in her eyes. Her bottom lip quivered. "You really mean that?"

"Yes. From the first moment I heard about you I couldn't wait until I found you. I wished I had known thirteen years ago, but I didn't." *And I've finally gotten past that.* "I figure better late than never." He tried to grin but the sight of her glistening eyes pierced his heart. What if she didn't want him in her life? What would he do?

"You're gonna stay in Tallgrass?"

"Yep. I've moved around a lot in the past fifteen years, but not anymore."

A tear rolled down her face. Taylor sniffed and swiped her hand across her cheek. "I'd like to get to know you better. Maybe we could do a few things together."

"Sounds like a plan to me." Hope flared in him. Hope that he could have a relationship with his daughter. Hope that he could persuade Rachel he loved her and wanted them to be a true family.

Taylor rubbed her hands across her eyes. "Well, I'd better go."

The urge to hug her overwhelmed him, but he knew he had to take it slow. A week ago that would have frustrated him. Not now. He could build on this start tonight.

He followed Taylor to his front door and opened it. Turning in the entrance, she smiled, her expression bright with—hope.

"I'll see you tomorrow, Max."

Maybe one day she would call him dad. "Good night." He observed her until she went into her house across the street. After talking with her, he knew what he had to do now. Closing the door, he headed for his phone to start making plans.

"Why aren't you and Zachary doing something special this evening? It'll be your first New Year's Eve together." Rachel finished packing Will's backpack with his pajamas and a change of clothes.

Jordan stuffed Sam's bag with an extra outfit for tomorrow. "This isn't our first New Year's Eve together. Remember we dated in high school. And we are doing something special. We're gonna be with family. All the kids are gonna spend the night at Becca's and stay up late."

"Are you sure about Will and Sam going?"

"Yep. They'll be five soon and I hate leaving them out of the fun. You can come if you want."

Rachel shook her head. "I'd be a fifth wheel. It would be nice to be home alone for a while and get…" Do what? Mope around?

"Get your life in order?"

"Something like that. Taylor spent part of the day with Max and had a great time. They went grocery shopping. She's never had fun grocery shopping with me. Well, maybe when she was four or five."

"I'm a phone call away if you change your mind." Jordan grabbed both boys' backpacks.

Rachel made her way into the hallway. "I wouldn't be good company. Maybe I'll start taking down the Christmas decorations. The kids love to put them up but hate to help take them down. I don't blame them."

"Sorta like when I cook. I love to prepare a meal but hate to clean up. Zachary is good at that, thankfully. We're a team when it comes to dinner."

Team. She wanted that again. With Max. But all she had heard about him these past few days was through her daughter.

Downstairs, the children were waiting in the foyer, their faces full of excitement.

"What took ya so long?" Sam opened the front door and raced out on to the porch.

"Oh, look, it's snowing." Taylor slung her backpack over her shoulder. "This is gonna be the best New Year's Eve."

"I get the front seat." Will shot ahead of his two siblings, running for Jordan's car.

"I'll bring them back tomorrow afternoon." Jordan hugged Rachel, then hurried after the trio as the snow began to fall in earnest.

Rachel turned to go back into her house when she caught sight of Kevin pulling up to her mother's. Telling Mom and Granny about Max and Taylor hadn't been as hard as she'd thought. Her mother hadn't even been surprised. She'd said she'd known something was going on, and when she thought about it, Max and Taylor looked alike. Her mother never liked surprises or changes so for her to take it so calmly had to be because of Kevin. His influence had been good for her mother.

Before she closed the front door, her gaze fell on Max's place. Lights blazed from it. What was he doing for New Year's Eve? Taylor said he had plans for the evening but short of interrogating her daughter she didn't know what those plans were.

Back in the warm confines of her house, Rachel ambled toward the kitchen to grab something to eat. As she examined the contents of her refrigerator, the chimes echoed through her home. Maybe one of her kids forgot something. She hurried into the foyer. When she looked out the peephole and saw Max, her heartbeat responded by accelerating.

When she reached for the door, her hand quaked so much her fingers slipped on the knob. She tried again and finally opened it. "Hi," was all she could think of saying as she took in his casual attire of black jeans and turtleneck under his unzipped leather coat. Then her gaze settled on what he was carrying—a basket.

"In case you forgot, I owe you one catered dinner. I'm here to deliver it."

"What if I have already eaten?"

"You haven't."

"How do you know?"

"Taylor. She's my spy." He winked and moved into her foyer, his bearing commanding, confident.

"Spy? Are we at war or something?" Her question came out breathless because her heart wouldn't keep from beating so fast.

"Or something. I'm here to negotiate a truce—a lifetime one."

A lifetime? She shut the door, glancing at the blanket of snow now covering the ground. Its freshness lent a newness to the landscape, sparking a seed of hope deep within her. "What did you fix?"

"Your favorite or at least according to your family. Prime roast beef, scalloped potatoes and asparagus in a special lemon sauce. Then for dessert I have a chocolate torte with whipped cream. I had to go to several stores to get the best ingredients."

"So, this is what you and Taylor were doing today. And my daughter kept it a secret. Not like her. She usually blurts it out the first chance she can get."

"She wanted this to be a surprise."

"It is. Where do you want to eat?"

"In front of the fireplace. I'll build a fire."

"I could have one going now."

"You don't."

"Taylor again?"

"Yep." Max headed back to the den as if it were his house.

She trailed after him, breathing in deep inhalations of air to calm her maddening heartbeat. "So, you and Taylor are getting along all right?"

"We are building a relationship that I hope will extend for years to come."

"Knowing you it will." Which meant she had to deal with him being in her life. Seeing him this evening, relaxed and carefree, made her realize that would be difficult.

He got the fire started then knelt by the basket on the circular rug in front of the hearth. The aromas of the roast beef and other dishes wafted to her. Her stomach growled its hunger. His economical movements as he laid out the feast mesmerized her—like an indoor picnic.

"You said my family told you my favorite food. Did you talk to everyone about what you were doing?"

"Yep. I wanted to make sure you were here alone tonight."

"Why?"

He straightened, only a foot away from her. "Because I want to convince you that I love you—not just Taylor or even your boys. You. Rachel, I love you. I did the day you asked me."

She wanted to believe his words. He'd probably convinced himself he did, but how could she know it was really true? "Have you forgiven Alicia?"

"A few days ago I talked with Pastor John. I left there and thought about what he'd said. I finally let go of my anger at Alicia that day, but I wanted to be sure before I said anything to you. You deserve someone who is totally committed to you. Who isn't living in the past, hanging on to something that was eating at him." He clasped her upper arms. "I can honestly say I have. When I think about Alicia, my stomach doesn't tighten."

The feel of his fingers on her nearly robbed her of coherent thought. But this was too important not to think rationally. "You've moved on?"

His hands grazed a path to her shoulders, and he gently tugged her toward him, nestling her against him. "Not only have I moved on, I'm ready to begin the rest of my life with you."

"How do I know you haven't just convinced yourself that you love me because of Taylor?"

"Maybe this will," he murmured close to her mouth, his breath scented with peppermint.

His fingers delved into her hair, holding her head still while his lips settled on hers in a possession that rocked her to her core. Nothing else mattered in that moment. His arms locked about her, his hands stroking the length of her back. In that mating of mouths he poured his heart into it, reaching deep inside her to show her how he felt about her.

When they parted, she swayed toward him, and he steadied her. Dazed by his powerful persuasion, all she could do was stare into his green eyes, the color of a sun-kissed meadow, and think she never wanted to leave his embrace.

"Do you need any more convincing that I love you? Yes, I love Taylor, but what I feel for you is totally different."

Still she hesitated, more from the stunned overwhelming emotions of love flowing through her than anything else.

"Remember, Rachel, you haven't denied me seeing Taylor, and that's one of the many reasons I love you. I suppose us being married might make it a little easier for me to see my daughter, but if I still felt the same about getting married as before, do you really think I would do it just to be in the same house as Taylor?"

Finally rallying to her senses, she smiled. "You had me with that kiss. Actually, I think you had me when you held up the basket of food."

His mouth curved upward, his eyes sparkling. "Does that mean you'll marry me?"

"If I said no, I have a feeling my daughter wouldn't be too happy."

He chuckled. "Not to mention me. You don't know how much trouble I went to coordinating this evening. And Granny made me promise to call her if you said yes."

"Then you'd better, or she'll be over here."

Max strolled to the phone on the desk and called Granny, letting it ring over a minute. "She's not there?"

"She should be. Her and Doug were staying in for New Year's Eve."

The doorbell rang. Max looked at Rachel and threw back his head, laughing. "Most impatient."

"That's Granny." Rachel headed to the front door and answered it.

Standing in the entrance were Granny and Doug, bundled up against the snow. "Well, what did you say, child?"

Barely containing her amusement, Rachel raised an eyebrow. "To what?"

Granny peered over Rachel's shoulder. "Don't tell me, young man, you didn't make your move." She dug into her coat pocket, retrieved a sheet of paper and waved it in the air. "If you ever want to see the fudge recipe, you'd better hop to it."

"Have you ever heard of leading up to the big moment?" Max asked, laughter still tingeing his voice.

"Not Helen. She didn't give me a chance to ask her to marry her. She asked me." Doug snatched the paper from his wife's hand and held it out to Max, who took it. "I can see by Rachel's look you asked and she said yes."

"Well, in that case, I expect to get the sweet potato casserole recipe in return." Granny gave Max a stern look, but within the narrowed eyes was a twinkle.

"That's fair. I'll get it to you tomorrow."

Rachel pushed the door open wide. "Come in and get warm."

"No way, child. This is our first New Year's Eve together. We're going home to smooch. I got what I came for." Granny grabbed Doug's hand and turned to leave.

Max slipped his arm around Rachel, leaned close to her ear and said, "I can picture us like that in forty years."

Rachel rested her head on his shoulder. "Yeah." She glanced up at him. "I guess we don't have to let the rest of the family know I've agreed to marry you. Granny will take care of that the second she gets home."

Max moved back and closed the door. "Then all we have to do is celebrate the coming of a brand-new year. A year of great possibilities." Taking her into his embrace, he sealed that declaration with a kiss.

Epilogue

The crack of the bat connecting with the softball echoed through the ballpark. Rachel lumbered to her feet and cheered as Taylor rounded the bases in a home run, the biggest grin on her face. Max came out of the dugout and scooped his daughter up into his arms, twirling her around.

"She did it. They won," Jordan said next to Rachel in the bleachers.

"Yep, she did, but I suspect the best thing today is that Max is here to see it."

"Of course he is. He's the coach. Well, the assistant."

Rachel shifted toward her sister. "She's always loved playing softball, but this season has been special. When Max agreed to help the coach, she floated around the house for days."

"And later today we get to celebrate her fifteenth birthday. Mom will be back from her elopement and can tell us why she went to Las Vegas to get married instead of here. I could throttle her."

"I don't think she wanted any fuss over her marriage to Kevin, but we'll get her back next weekend with the surprise wedding reception. She can't think she'd get married and we not celebrate it with her." Rachel spied Taylor and Max heading toward her.

"It took her long enough. I thought she would never marry Kevin. A year and a half. And poor Granny. She tried everything to get them together faster."

Rachel laughed. "Granny thought she'd lost her touch. I think Mom delayed her marriage just to needle Granny."

"The team is going out for pizza to celebrate winning the championship. I'm riding with Ashley. Okay?" Taylor gave Rachel her softball mitt.

"Fine. Prairie Pizza Parlor?"

"Yeah." Taylor started back toward the group of teen-age girls surrounding the main coach of the Cowgirl team. She stopped after several feet and turned back. "Dad, aren't ya coming?"

"I'll be there in a sec. You go enjoy your victory." When he faced Rachel, a look of happiness radiated from him. "How are you doing—" he glanced down at her protruding stomach "—and little Beth?"

"We're doing fine, but if she doesn't come soon, I'm going to have a talk with her about keeping us waiting."

"It won't be the last time if our daughter is any indication."

"Yeah, Taylor has never gotten the hang of being on time."

"Dad," Taylor shouted.

Max gave Rachel a quick kiss. "I'd better get over there. This is a big deal. Their first championship." He jogged toward the team lining up on the field.

At that moment, a pain sliced through Rachel's stomach. Suddenly, she felt a warm rush of liquid and looked down. "My water broke."

Jordan leaped up. "I'll go get Max. Do you have your bags packed? Are they in the car?"

"Let him and Taylor enjoy this moment." Rachel fixed her gaze on her husband and daughter, standing arm in arm while the official presented the trophy to the team.

They were a family eager to welcome a new member into it.

* * * * *

Dear Reader,

I can't believe I've come to the end of my homeschooling series for Love Inspired. I really enjoyed exploring the different reasons and situations that might lead to a parent deciding to homeschool. Of course, there were others I didn't get to show. But it is an option for some children. When dealing with a child, we need to look at the individual and decide what is best for that child. Our children are our future.

I love hearing from readers. You can contact me a margaretdaley@gmail.com or at P.O. Box 2074 Tulsa, OK 74101. You can also learn more about my books at http://www.margaretdaley.com. I have a quarterly newsletter that you can sign up for on my website or you can enter my monthly drawings by signing my guest book on the website.

Best wishes,

Margaret Daley

QUESTIONS FOR DISCUSSION

1. Taylor has Attention Deficit Disorder with Hyperactivity. Do you know anyone who has this? What are some things you can do to help a person with ADHD?

2. Who is your favorite character? Why?

3. When Max came to Tallgrass, he didn't know how he was going to proceed with Taylor. What would you have done in this situation?

4. Rachel's husband died two and a half years before. She still wore her wedding ring, and when she took it off it was a hard decision for her. Have you been in a similar situation? What would make you take off your wedding ring after your husband/wife died?

5. What is your favorite scene? Why?

6. To Rachel, her wedding ring was a symbol of Lawrence and their marriage. Do you have a symbol or item that is important to you? Why does it mean so much to you?

7. Max couldn't forgive Alicia for what she had done to him. Have you been unable to forgive someone? Why?

8. What is your favorite Bible verse on forgiveness? Why?

9. Max let his past control his present, his actions. Have

you ever been controlled by something in your past? Were you able to put it behind you? How?

10. Eileen Masterson, Rachel's mother, was upset Granny was marrying and moving out. She was lonely and didn't want to see Granny get married and leave her. How do you deal with loneliness?

11. Rachel felt out of her element dealing with Taylor and her situation. Have you ever felt that way? What have you done about it?

12. What does Christmas mean to you?

13. Taylor was upset because she thought she was dumb. She got angry, especially with her mother, because Taylor didn't know how to deal with her feelings. What are some things she could have done to deal with her anger?

14. Max didn't celebrate Christmas because he worked on that day. He didn't have any traditions. What is your favorite Christmas memory/tradition?

15. What are some reason parents would homeschool their child? Have you homeschooled a child? Would you consider doing it? Why or why not?

TITLES AVAILABLE NEXT MONTH

Available November 30, 2010

AN AMISH CHRISTMAS
Brides of Amish Country
Patricia Davids

THE LAWMAN'S CHRISTMAS WISH
Alaskan Bride Rush
Linda Goodnight

JINGLE BELL BLESSINGS
Rosewood, Texas
Bonnie K. Winn

YULETIDE COWBOY
Men of Mule Hollow
Debra Clopton

THE HOLIDAY NANNY
Lois Richer

MONTANA HEARTS
Charlotte Carter

LICNM1110